ALSO BY JULIE B COSGROVE

Wordplay Mysteries

Word Has It
Word Gets Around
In Other Words
Hang on Every Word (coming soon)

Relatively Seeking Mysteries

One Leaf Too Many
Fallen Leaf
Leaf Me Alone

Bunco Biddies Series

Dumpster Dicing
Baby Bunco
Threes, Sixes & Thieves
'Til Dice Do Us Part

In Other Words

by

Julie B Cosgrove

Write Integrity Press, LLC

In Other Words

ISBN: 978-1-951602-11-6

Published by Pursued Books:
an imprint of Write Integrity Press, LLC
PO Box 702852
Dallas, TX 75370

Find out more about the author, Julie B Cosgrove,
at her website: www.juliebcosgrove.com
or on her author page at www.WriteIntegrity.com.

Printed in the United States of America.

Dedication

Do not lie to each other,
since you have taken off your old self
with its practices and have put on the new self,
which is being renewed
in knowledge in the image of its Creator . . .
Christ is all, and is in all.
Colossians 3:9,11b

"No matter how far
you have traveled in the wrong direction,
you can always turn around."
- Manthan Sharma

Dedicated to those who have
had the courage to turn around
and turn to Jesus.

Contents

Cast of Characters

Wanda Lee Warner – A widow who loves word games. She has lived in Scrub Oak, TX most of her life. Has a natural curiosity about events in her town because she loves her community and its residents. She has a dachshund named Sophie.

Betty Sue Simpson – Wanda's best friend since they were kids. She is also a widow. As a retired elementary school teacher, she knows the background of almost everyone who has lived in town since 1965. She also likes word games and puzzles.

Evelyn Joseph – Wanda's next-door neighbor. She moved to Scrub Oak ten years ago to care for her sister until she passed from cancer. The widow of an Army Intelligence officer, who was killed in the Gulf War in 1990, she never remarried. She stayed in Scrub Oak because she and Wanda became good friends and she wanted to finally put down roots.

Todd Martin – Wanda's nephew, who has returned to Scrub Oak to join the police force. They have always been close and enjoy a good game of Scrabble together on Thursday mornings before his shift. He lived with his aunt during his high school years after his parents divorced.

Hazel Perks – a neighbor who lives near the old, abandoned Ferguson Mansion and is an avid gardener. It also keeps her aware of the goings on in her neighborhood. She grows prize roses.

Fred Ballinger – the retired principal of the Scrub Oak's lower school. He has eyes for Betty Sue.

Priscilla Tucker – owns the Coffee Bean, a local coffee shop that sells organic roasts from all over the world. Her sister, Sally, ran Sally's Salads which also featured the organic blends.

Sally Ibson – owns Sally's Salads where she also serves breakfast breads and coffee from her sister's Coffee Bean.

Shari Wright – Sally and Priscilla's younger sister who had a sordid life but is trying to turn it around. In charge of the organic section in the Grocery Mart.

Collin Rollins –is a neighborhood watch captain and owns the Grocery Mart. His wife **Claudia** owns and runs A Cut Above, a barber/beauty salon that plays only Christian contemporary songs.

Isaac Rollins – stock manager at the Grocery Mart. He is Collin and Claudia's son.

Angie Espinosa – is a longtime, loyal employee at the Grocery Mart. She greets customers with a smile when she is the cashier.

Miguel Garza – Produce Manager at the Grocery Mart. He and Isaac have known each other since ninth grade. His father, Manuel, owns the liquor store.

Manuel Garza – owns the liquor store. He opened it a few years ago after tiring of his commute to Fort Worth for thirty years managing one there.

Chief Brooks – the police chief of Scrub Oak. All business and a stickler for rules, but underneath he has a soft heart.

Pastor Bob Thomas – the clergyman at Holy Hill Church where Wanda attends.

Tom Jacobs – owner of Tom's Thrift Shop and local editor for the *Oakmont County Weekly Gazette*. His wife is **Misty Jacobs.** His grown daughter is **Vicki Jacobs** (now Mrs. Mason Clyburn).

Mason Clyburn – Vicki's new husband. He helps run the Gazette and is the business manager of Tom's Thrift Shop.

Mary Lou Fitzgerald – a new mother with a baby named **Lucy**. She is the organist at Holy Hill and was a high school teacher.

Frank Patterson – a nice old guy with COPD from years of smoking foul-smelling stogies. He lives behind Wanda. Quiet, but his eyes see a lot that goes on. Now he sucks on thick pretzel sticks and always has one in his mouth.

Finn and Emma Mae Buckley – live across the street from Frank. She is the receptionist at Schiller and Smith. Finn, an extraordinary handyman, works odd jobs around town. Everyone calls him Fix-it Finn.

Melissa Suntych – an artist who lives on the edge of town off Woodway Drive and rescues animals, domestic and wild. She and her husband, **Jerry**, are on the neighborhood watch.

Henry Hampton – Owner of Hardware Haven.

Scrub Oak, TX

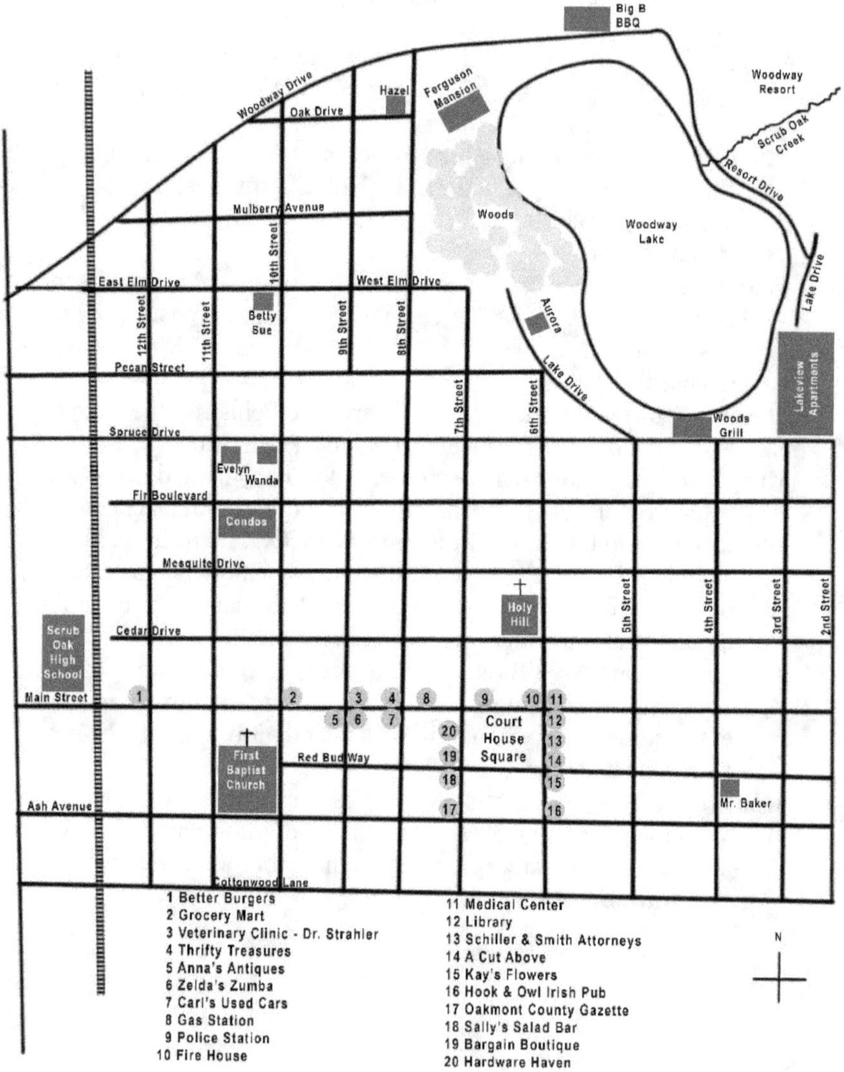
Big B BBQ
Woodway Resort
Scrub Oak Creek
Resort Drive
Woodway Drive
Oak Drive
Hazel
Ferguson Mansion
Woods
Woodway Lake
Lake Drive
Mulberry Avenue
10th Street
East Elm Drive
West Elm Drive
12th Street
11th Street
Betty Sue
9th Street
8th Street
Aurora
Lakeview Apartments
Pecan Street
7th Street
6th Street
Woods Grill
Spruce Drive
Evelyn
Wanda
Fir Boulevard
Condos
Mesquite Drive
Holy Hill
5th Street
4th Street
3rd Street
2nd Street
Scrub Oak High School
Cedar Drive
Main Street
Court House Square
First Baptist Church
Red Bud Way
Ash Avenue
Mr. Baker
Cottonwood Lane
N
1 Better Burgers
2 Grocery Mart
3 Veterinary Clinic - Dr. Strahler
4 Thrifty Treasures
5 Anna's Antiques
6 Zelda's Zumba
7 Carl's Used Cars
8 Gas Station
9 Police Station
10 Fire House
11 Medical Center
12 Library
13 Schiller & Smith Attorneys
14 A Cut Above
15 Kay's Flowers
16 Hook & Owl Irish Pub
17 Oakmont County Gazette
18 Sally's Salad Bar
19 Bargain Boutique
20 Hardware Haven

Chapter One

“I’ve discovered how to not get stressed.” Wanda Lee Warner leaned back in her kitchen dinette chair and tried to hide the smile that wanted to spread across her cheeks.

“Really?” Betty Sue, her almost life-long friend, glanced up from studying her letter tiles as her eyes widened. “And that is?”

“Turn it around.” Wanda spun the Scrabble board so that the letters appeared upside down. She pointed to each letter. “Desserts. Get it? Reduce stress by eating desserts.”

Betty Sue cocked her head to read it. Then she scoffed. “Honestly, Wanda. If I ate desserts again, I’d gain back all the weight I lost and then get stressed about it.”

Wanda chuckled and twisted the playing board back to face Betty Sue.

“But you’re right, Wanda. It is funny how many words can be spelled the same frontward and backward.”

“Okay, retired teacher. There is a name for that, isn’t there?”

"Well, yes..." Betty Sue paused to rearrange some of the letters on her slate. "A palindrome is a word like pop, dad, or mom. However, a phrase liked 'stressed desserts' would be one as well."

"I get it."

"Do you know what's the world's longest palindrome?" Her friend's eyes twinkled with mischief.

"No. Tell me." Wanda's interest perked. She loved words and word puzzles. Perhaps she should have been a teacher as well. Or a detective. After all, in the past year she had helped solve several murders and burglaries in Scrub Oak, Texas, their small town forty-five minutes south of Fort Worth.

"It's saippuakivikauppias." Betty Sue peered over her reading glasses with a smug professor expression.

"What?" Wanda scrunched her nose. "Spell it."

Betty Sue took her pen and wrote the word out on her score pad. It was so long she had to wrap it around the corner and down the side.

"Is that real word?" Wanda tried to mouth it out.

"Yes. It is for a person who deals in lye."

"As in falsehoods?"

"No, Wanda. L-y-e. Like tanning hides. It is Finnish, as in from Finland, not as in completing something."

Wanda swatted at her hand. "Betty Sue Simpson, I'll tan your hide. It's not even English."

She chuckled and got up to pour herself another cup of

coffee from Wanda's machine. "You know, this new Kenya blend from the Coffee Bean is really good. Priscilla is getting better in her selections."

"I think after the lavender coffee crime, she has realized that us small town folk don't have the same palate as those millennials in the Metroplex."

"True." Betty Sue set her cup down with a thud, which jolted Sophie, Wanda's dachshund, from a sound sleep in her bed by the fridge. "Say, why don't we head over to the Grocery Mart and order a skinny latte. Then we can check out the premiere opening of the organic section. Sally and Priscilla's little sister is running it."

Wanda gawked. "I didn't know that. Neither she nor Priscilla ever said a thing."

"Uh, huh. Shari Wright. She hasn't always led a stellar life, got into drugs and all that."

"That's a shame. So how . . .?"

Betty Sue brought the mug to her lips, then set it down again. "Brief prison time along with rehab where she began to study organics and herbs."

"I see." Then the new section would be perfect for her.

Betty Sue smiled and lifted her cup in a toast. "And she met Jesus there as well, Sally told me. She accepted Him as her Savior, received forgiveness, went back to school, and got a degree in holistic nutrition." She nodded and finally took a gulp her coffee.

Wanda waited, sensing there was more to the story.

Betty Sue wiped her mouth and folded the paper napkin in thirds. "Last month Priscilla and Sally convinced Collin to give Shari a chance. He's put her in charge of this new organic produce and products section. Today is opening day."

"Hmm. Well, let's go check it out." Wanda rose and pushed in her chair. Anything new happening in her town always sparked her attention.

"Good. I want to get some spaghetti squash."

"Spaghetti squash?"

"A healthy substitute for pasta. Don't scrunch your nose, Wanda. I'll cook some up for supper and invite you over to taste test it."

"Well, all right. I'll try it. Once." Wanda grabbed her purse, patted Sophie's head, and followed Betty Sue out the backdoor.

No one in Scrub Oak used the front door unless they were selling something or coming for their date. Though, after the recent crime spree, most of the residents had started locking their doors. One of the reasons Wanda helped organize a neighborhood watch program. But secretly she admitted to herself she did it to assist her nephew, Todd Martin. She wanted to prove his worth as a budding police officer in town. And recently, after helping to solve two crime sprees, she had accomplished that goal.

The two women chatted as they walked the half-mile trek to the Grocery Mart. "A year ago, I would have hopped in my car. I never knew walking could be so refreshing, Betty Sue. I'm not even out of breath yet."

Her friend grinned as they crossed the parking lot, but not in an I-told-you-so way. One of the things Wanda loved about Betty Sue—her gentle spirit and kind heart, no matter what life tossed in her direction. Knowing her for over fifty-five years only made Wanda admire her even more. They paused outside the Grocery Mart to eye the stenciled signs on the plate-glass windows announcing the week's specials.

A siren's whoop-woo-whoop blasted behind them. The two women jumped onto the curb, hands to their hearts.

Jimmy Bob's police cruiser zipped by them down 10th Street at an alarming speed. More sirens began to whine, coming from the east in the direction of the fire station.

"What on earth?' Wanda quickened her pace to a jog, with Betty Sue falling in sync with her strides.

Up ahead they saw swirling red lights bounce off the tree trunks that lined the side street.

Betty Sue pointed. "It appears to be coming from the alley behind the grocery store."

Wanda slowed her steps when she saw her nephew, who should be off duty, cordon off the entrance with crime tape. Oh, no. Not again. Not in her town.

"Todd, Todd! What's going on?"

He glanced up but continued in his task. "You need to leave, Aunt Wanda. You as well, Betty Sue."

"Why?" Wanda peeked around his shoulder. A petite,

slumped figure lay in the alleyway amidst a few toppled boxes of veggies. Its long black hair draped over the asphalt. A slim trail of crimson oozed from the direction of the head.

A piercing wail of agony echoed from the grocer's back entrance.

Betty Sue and Wanda gasped at the sight of Sally and Priscilla clinging to each other, their shoulders heaving in sorrow. Collin stood to the side and rubbed the back of his neck, his face as pale as Hazel Perks' prize-winning snowcap roses.

As the EMT's gingerly flipped and placed the limp body onto a gurney, Betty Sue whispered through her hand clasped to her mouth. "Oh, my heavens. It's Shari."

Four Cheese Spaghetti Squash Boats

Ingredients:

- 3 Tbsp salted butter
- 3 cloves garlic, minced, or 1 tsp of garlic powder
- 3 Tbsp all-purpose flour
- 1/2 c. milk
- 1/2 c. bone broth - I use chicken bone broth.
- 1/2 c. shredded mozzarella
- 1/2 c. finely shredded fresh Parmesan, not grated
- 1/3 c. shredded provolone

- 1/3 c. shredded fontina
- 1 Tbsp dried green chives
- 3 Crisp bacon strips crumbled
- Sea salt
- White pepper
- 4 spaghetti squash, halved and seeded
- 1/4 c. Avocado oil
- Chopped fresh parsley, for garnish

Directions:

1. Preheat the oven to 400 degrees.
2. Cut the squashes in half then using a spoon, scoop out the seeds. Rub the outsides with avocado oil. (I dab it on with a paper towel, but you can use your hands if you like.) Sprinkle sea salt and pepper on each of the inside of the halves then place them face down on a foil-wrapped cookie sheet.
3. Bake for 40 minutes then remove them from the oven to cool enough to handle.
4. Over medium heat so it doesn't smoke, melt the butter in a large skillet. Stir in the garlic. If using fresh cloves, stir until they become fragrant. Next, use a whisk to blend in the flour until the mixture is golden colored. Finally, slowly pour in the milk and broth, stirring constantly.
5. Combine the cheese, chives, and bacon crumbles in a large bowl. Scoop out ½ cup to use as the topping then add the rest to the skillet. Add the salt and pepper. Wisk everything until smooth and creamy,

then remove from the heat.

6. Scoop out the "spaghetti" strands from the cooled squash halves with a fork and add them to the skillet mixture. Blend well then spoon the mixture into the shelled-out halves and place them back on the foil-wrapped cookie sheet.
7. Sprinkle the reserved cheese, chives and bacon crumble mix evenly on the top of each. Turn the broiler on high and broil until golden, but no longer than two-three minutes.

Betty Sue likes it garnished with a sprig of curly parsley on top.

Chapter Two

Todd swung around. "You know her then, Betty Sue?"

"Only met her day before yesterday. She's Priscilla and Sally's younger sister."

Todd nodded. "Yeah, she just moved into Lakeway Apartments this past weekend. One building down from me. Hadn't really met her though."

Wanda watched the EMTs lift the person into the back of the van. "At least they didn't cover her face. She is alive then, I assume."

"Yes. Unconscious but alive." A long sigh blasted from Todd's lips.

Wanda understood. A few months ago, her other good friend, Evelyn, also lay in an alley with a head injury, but her assault happened behind the headquarters of the *Oakmont County Weekly Gazette* after she stumbled onto a crime. The place had been ransacked and Tom Jacobs lay unconscious on the floor. Why did this continue to happen in their peaceful little town?

They watched as the ambulance left the scene in the opposite direction, beyond the flapping yellow tape. Its pulsated warning sound revved up, something it rarely did for the short four-block ride to the Medical Center. Wanda surmised they were taking the victim to the county hospital up the highway. If they were, then their passenger needed more special care than their little community could offer.

Oh, dear.

Jimmy Bob sat in his cruiser chatting over the squawk box, no doubt to Chief Brooks. Even with cell phones, they still did some things the old-fashioned way. Todd once told her most police still prefer dispatch channels to spread the word because then several can listen in and respond.

Wanda touched his shoulder. “You do know about her past, right? She was in rehab for drugs.”

“Oh? And you know this because? Oh, never mind. Half the town probably does by now.” He scuffed the alley floor with his boot. “Welcome to Scrub Oak where your business is everyone else’s.”

He trudged away, leaving Wanda and Betty Sue on the spectator side of the yellow tape.

Wanda crossed her arms. “He’s in a foul mood.”

“Well, dear. It’s only nine something in the morning. He was probably asleep. He had the overnight shift as usual, right?”

“Yeah. Still. Something else is bugging him. I can tell.”

“It couldn’t possibly be because another crime has

infested our community?" A touch of snark dripped from her words.

Wanda swung to stare at her usually Pollyanna-like friend. It was uncharacteristic of her to have such an attitude.

Betty Sue's cheeks reddened. "Sorry. Guess it is getting to me, too." She swiped a tear from her eye. "I really liked Shari the moment we met at Zelda's Zumba. All she wanted was a new start. Who would do such a thing? Poor Sally and Priscilla."

"I don't know." Wanda glanced at the two sisters with grief and shock plastered on their faces. Behind them, Todd pulled Collin aside for a private conversation. What Wanda wouldn't give to hear them.

Then Betty Sue did another uncharacteristic thing. The retired schoolteacher, who always obeyed the rules to the letter, ducked under the cordon and dashed over to hug her friends.

What else could Wanda do but follow? She huffed and scooted under the tape as well.

Priscilla wobbled, then crouched on the back stoop, shivering. Sally draped her arm around her as Betty Sue bent down to rub her back in soft circular motions.

"What happened?" Wanda joined the huddled women.

Priscilla swiped the running mascara from the crescents under her eyes, making them appear even darker. "We don't know."

Sally shaded her eyes from the morning sun as she gazed up at Wanda. “I came to pick up some more kale, cherry tomatoes, and green leaf lettuce from Shari. We had agreed that from now on I would only serve organics at my salad bar, and that she and Collin would supply them. That was part of the deal that convinced him to give this a try.” She let loose of a slight shudder and then continued. “When I got here a little before nine, Shari was in a tither. Only half of her stock had arrived yesterday after closing.”

Priscilla glanced up. “We spent half the night setting things up, along with Shari, Collin, and Isaac. But more was to be delivered this morning.”

“And it never came?” A shivery sensation crept up Wanda’s arms.

Priscilla gazed into space with hollow eyes. “It was scheduled to arrive at seven o’clock, a full hour before the grand opening. Shari had been on the phone with the dispatch most of the morning, and they had yet to hear from the driver.”

“Weird.” Wanda puckered her brow and scanned the scene of toppled vegetables.

Sally swallowed loud enough for Wanda to hear over the hushed conversations between Collin and Todd, which she tried to pick up with her other ear. Not to much avail, though. Maybe she did need to get her hearing tested. Was sixty-two too young to develop hearing loss?

Her thoughts returned to Sally’s voice.

"We heard what sounded like a truck's engine chugging down the alley. Shari rushed out to greet it."

"And probably to give the driver a piece of her mind." Priscilla nodded as she wrung a tissue through her fingers before dabbing her eyes again.

"Our little sister had a temper at times. Diplomacy was not her strong suit." Sally dug in her purse for a fresh Kleenex and handed it to Priscilla.

Priscilla took it, blew her nose, and then moaned. "Then we heard her scream followed by a loud thud. We ran to the back door, which had been swung wide open, and found her slumped over the produce . . ." She paused to take in a deep breath of air. "Unconscious. Oh, why?"

Wanda peered down the back street. "Where is the delivery truck now?"

Before anyone could answer, if they could that is, the county forensic van pulled up and a team draped in paper suits and gloves piled out to begin processing the scene. They shuffled around tagging things, clicking cameras, and murmuring to each other.

Todd trotted over to his aunt. "I told you not to come in here. This is . . ."

"I know. A crime scene. And you don't want evidence tampered with."

He pressed his lips together until they paled. Yes, something had gotten under his skin. She hoped it wasn't her...again. She opened her mouth to ask him but halted at the sound of the police chief arriving with a screech of tires.

Then something caught her eye. Above the crates appeared some graffiti, hastily sprayed from the looks of it. Collin prided himself on neatness and cleanliness when it came to his grocery store, inside and out. He'd never let anything like that stay on his brick walls for long.

"Isn't this new?" She pointed to the green scrawl with small runs dribbling from it.

Todd swiveled on his boot heel and shoved his khaki police Stetson back off his brow. "Hey, Jimmy Bob. Tell forensics to get a photo of this. Okay?"

Then he stepped closer, and Wanda followed in his shadow.

With gloved hands, Todd lifted two crates of veggies out of the way.

Wanda read it out loud. "I did, did I?" A quiver went up Wanda's spinal column, chilling each vertebra. "Oh, my word. I don't believe it."

Todd eyed her. "What?"

"It's a palindrome."

"A what?"

"Pal-in-drome. Like pop, radar, mom. See?"

His face still registered incomprehension.

Betty Sue joined the conversation. "In other words, it is a word or group of words that read the same forward and backward." She pointed to the wall art. "Your aunt and I were just talking about that this morning as we played

Scrabble."

Todd shook his head. "Weird."

"I know." Wanda shuddered and cast her attention to Betty Sue. From her expression, Wanda could tell she thought the same thing. This did not appear to be a coincidence.

Her Scrabble board had helped them discover clues in the last two crime sprees. It appeared to be doing it again. It was as if God had tasked them with solving yet another one.

But what did the palindrome mean?

Who did what, did they? Was someone confessing a crime or denying their involvement? She had no clue. But she planned to find out with the help of her neighbors and the police. This wasn't her first rodeo, as the saying goes. Her sleuthing had helped bring perps to justice before.

Wanda silently prayed they'd solve this mystery soon. Crime had become way too frequent a thing in this North Texas town. As head of the neighborhood watch association, that prickled her conscience.

Time for these crimes in her community to stop. She'd do what she could to make sure they did. She picked up the proverbial gauntlet that whoever committed this crime had thrown down and claimed the challenge, with God's help.

Chapter Three

"This will simply not do."

Wanda ignored the arched eyebrow on her nephew and tugged on Betty Sue's arm. She led her a few steps away, hopefully out of earshot with all the other commotion in the alley.

"What does this all mean, Wanda?"

"I'm not sure." She tilted her head toward the graffiti. "But I don't believe in coincidences."

"Right? I mean less than an hour ago we were talking about palindromes and here one appears on the wall directly above where someone clobbered Shari."

Wanda would have laughed at Betty Sue's description of the crime at any other time. But not now. This was way too creepy not to be connected. She inched over to the wall and placed her finger on one of the paint drips. It felt cool to the touch and the slight odor of aerosol emitted from the droplet. Yep. It had been newly written.

"Hey, lady. Stop that." One of the forensic team pointed at her. Then he turned to Todd. "Get these people out of here."

Collin's face blanched as he turned toward the alley wall. His mouth opened, but no words exited. Wanda surmised by his expression that he had been too focused on Shari's condition to notice the desecrated wall of his grocery.

Todd whistled and waved his arms as if herding sheep. One by one, Collin, Betty Sue, Wanda, Priscilla, and Sally edged through the backdoor into the stocking section of the grocery store. A small crowd had stopped shopping and chatted among themselves as they peeked beyond the storeroom entrance toward the alleyway.

Collin pushed through the gathering "Everything is fine. Just a little accident that's being cleaned up. Please return to your shopping."

Wanda tried hard to not roll her eyes. Collin didn't exactly lie after all. But in this town, the whole truth would soon seep out like spilled organic, extra virgin olive oil onto a shiny linoleum floor.

Todd slipped in from the storeroom and closed the backdoor to the alley. "He's right, folks. No need for worry." He motioned with his hand for them to leave.

The bewildered bunch of shoppers began to go about their business.

Wanda felt pride swelling in her chest. Todd really had

obtained the respect of the community. They no longer pictured him as the lanky, nerdy high school kid of a tragic divorce. In fact, even if she said so herself, he had filled out quite nicely, and the contact lenses definitely brought out his handsome cheekbones and vivid blue, long-lashed eyes.

She lifted her index finger, now blotched with green. "Did you notice the paint had been freshly applied?"

He narrowed his eyes as he handed her an antibacterial wipe from a packet in his pocket. "Yeah, except I could figure it out without touching it and contaminating a possible piece of evidence. I had to explain the tell-tale fingerprint didn't belong to the artist but my over-inquisitive aunt."

"Sheesh. It's only spray paint." She rubbed her finger until her skin turned slightly red instead of green.

"Which had a meaningful message to you. Want to fill me in?"

"I did, Todd." She handed him back the wipe, much to his surprise.

He wadded it up and shoved it into his pant pocket along with the wrapper it had come in. "Let me guess. You two ladies were playing Scrabble and one of you spelled out this pal, um palin..."

"Palindrome." Betty Sue scooted up to him to join in the conversation. "And as we walked down here to check out Shari's section, we began reciting others as we thought of them."

Wanda bobbed her head. "Then lo and behold, one is scrawled on the Grocery Mart's wall where we were headed. Coincidence? I think not."

"You're lapsing into Shakespearean language. Always frightening." Todd chuckled. Then his expression waned. "And because one appeared on your Scrabble board, you have determined this is yet another crime clue and thus your permission to become involved, correct?"

"Well, in the other two cases, it proved true." Wanda winked. "God works in mysterious ways."

Todd pulled her to the side. Betty Sue seemed to take the hint and backed away a bit, studying the high shelves.

He waggled his finger millimeters in front of her nose. "Stand down, Aunt Wanda. I mean it."

She jutted her chin. "At least, let my neighborhood captains keep an eye out for any more graffiti. And for anyone who might have green paint splatters on their clothes or fingers."

Betty Sue cleared her throat to catch their attention and stepped closer. "Why don't I ask Fred if he knows of any high school kids who might have done this." Fred Ballinger had retired as the high school principal but kept his thumb on the pulse of the school district. Many of the parents still came to him for advice.

Todd conceded. "Very well. But let the authorities go about finding the culprit who conked Shari. Hopefully, she will regain consciousness soon and be able to describe him."

"Or her. Could be either gender. Remember the last case we weren't sure . . ."

He sucked in his breath. "Yes, I do. By the way, Tom Jacobs is coming out of rehab next week. Did you hear? He will be back parttime at the thrift shop but is still leaving *The Gazette* to Vicki and Mason to manage."

"That is good news." Betty Sue clasped her hands together. "I must say the newspaper has greatly improved under their leadership. Many folks agree."

"Better get back out there." Todd flashed them a brief smile, tipped his Stetson, and walked to the alley door.

Betty Sue swiveled on the balls of her tennis-shoed toes. "Well, what are we to do?"

"You console Priscilla. She still appears very pale." Wanda saw the woman frantically trying to serve people at her coffee bar in the front corner of the grocery store while probably answering their inquiries about her sister. Her eyes registered a growing frustration behind her professional customer service smile.

"Happy to." Betty Sue started in that direction but halted when Wanda grabbed her elbow.

"Then please call Fred. In the meantime, I am heading over to Hardware Haven to see if they have this color of paint in stock." She held up her middle finger then blushed at the obscene gesture she almost made.

Betty Sue giggled then play-punched Wanda's arm.

"You sly thing. You kept one finger from Todd's view."

Wanda winked. "Guilty."

Chapter Four

She strutted out the front door of the Grocery Mart as more townsfolk shuffled in. Not to do their weekly shopping as much as to snoop, she figured. Word had gotten around town already. Not exactly the advertising Collin would prefer. She didn't envy him. Perhaps tonight she should drop off a cheeseburger casserole for him and Claudia, his wife who ran the *A Cut Above* hair salon. The relaxing tone of that place with its Christian music always soothed her. The least she could do is attempt to soothe them back.

The hardware store lay two blocks away on 7th Street and Main, across from the courthouse square. Sally's Salad Bar sat two doors down. Wanda decided she'd bop in for lunch later to see how Shari's sister fared and get two salads to go for Collins and Claudia's dinner as well.

The old-fashioned bell on the hardware store's jamb tinkled when she entered. At the sound, another customer turned to see who had come in. Her backyard neighbor's eyes met hers.

"Hi, Frank. What brings you in here?"

He coughed. Frank always coughed. Too many years of sucking on cigarettes in his youth. She waited for the fit to settle so he could respond.

"Needed some wood screws for the side fence. I've decided to replace one side every spring. That way, in four years I will have a new fence all the way around. Cheaper than doing it all at once." He cleared his throat. "And you?"

"Looking for spray paint." She smiled and walked over to that aisle, leaving him to wonder why.

Frank had become the self-proclaimed eagle eye of the neighborhood. Maybe she should let him in on the current events, not that he wouldn't learn of it soon enough anyway.

She strolled back, chastising herself for her bout of snarkiness. "Truth is, Shari Wright, Priscilla and Sally's little sister, was accosted in the alley behind the Grocery Mart this morning."

"I heard. Is she okay?"

"Not sure. They took her to the county hospital."

He lowered his head and made a tsk-tsk sound.

"Anyway, close to where they found her slumped over, someone had freshly painted a graffiti message on the brick wall. I wanted to see if someone could have purchased the spray can here in town."

Frank's eyes glistened. "Aw. Madame Sleuth in action

once again."

She swatted away his comment, feeling her cheeks warm. "Only trying to help."

Henry Hampton shuffled over. "Can I assist either of you in finding anything?"

Fred gestured with a slight bow. "Ladies first."

Wanda thanked him then turned to the owner. "Yes, do you sell spray paint in this color?" This time, she turned her hand palm up to reveal the green on the tip of her middle finger. No way did she intend to make that faux pas gesture of holding it up again.

Henry lifted his glasses to stare at it then nodded rapidly. "Yes, we do. Right this way. An extremely popular color, you know."

Her hopes took a dive. "It is?"

"Oh, yes. Sell it all the time. Especially this time of year. People use it to freshen up their wrought iron furniture, their fences, flowerpots, you name it. Green means spring and we are almost there." He grinned wider.

"Of course. Well, have you sold any in the past day or so?"

He brought his eyebrows together in a question. "Of course. Mrs. Perks bought four cans yesterday."

Well, Hazel Perks hardly fit the profile of a graffiti artist. Wanda did recall her saying the green Victorian patio set counterbalanced the color of her prize roses though. Made them pop, as she put it.

Pop, another palindrome. Her mind returned to the sound of Henry's voice.

"Fix-it Finn bought a few. He is redoing the Suntych's rabbit hutches. Made sure it was non-toxic."

Right, another upstanding person in the community. "Anyone with kids?"

"Wanda, exactly what is this about?"

"Well, Henry. You may as well know. Someone sprayed green paint on the alley walls of the Grocery Mart."

He whistled. "I bet Collin is fit to be tied."

Frank laughed, which prompted another coughing spell. The poor man really needed respiratory therapy. Too proud to go, though.

Henry raised his voice a bit. "To answer your question, I can't honestly recall. But these cans last two to five years after they are opened. Could have been in someone's garage for quite a while."

Great. And few folks around here locked their garage doors. This clue seemed to be a dead end.

"Well, thanks, Henry."

"So, you don't want to buy a can then?" The man almost pouted.

Wanda thought about it, for a spilt-second. "Um, no. Not yet. I'll let you know."

She halted and eyed a rack of breath mints and gum next to the register. It would be rude not to buy something. After all, the man had a business to run. She chose a spearmint flavored mint and bought two packages.

Henry's demeanor brightened as she placed them on the counter and got out her coin purse. He thanked her as he rang up the purchases.

"Bye, neighbor." She waved at Frank whose concentration had turned to the wood screws.

He raised his hand without looking up.

As Wanda walked to Sally's for a quick bite, her brain wheels began to turn. Tonight, the neighborhood watch captains met to report on any incidents over the past two weeks. She'd almost forgotten they had changed the day of the week when they met. Land of mercy, this graffiti stuff had gotten to her more than she realized. Perhaps someone had recently complained of things missing from their garage. But until then, she could still find out a few things.

She called Hazel and asked her if she happened to have noticed any misplaced green cans of spray paint.

"Why?"

"Just wondering."

Hazel, also a widow, occasionally joined her, Betty Sue, and Evelyn in playing word games, as well as information-gathering now and then. Especially with a panoramic view of the Ferguson Mansion from her front yard where two murders had occurred.

"Now, Wanda, dear. Does this have anything to do about poor Shari Wright and the graffiti at the grocers?"

Wanda opened her mouth and then shut it. A blue jay

in the tree above her squawked a warning, and soon other birds began to tweet. Humans were not the only ones in Scrub Oaks that passed on the news in haste.

"As a matter of fact . . ."

"I knew it. I've been thinking. I hired Aaron Wallace to paint my patio set last weekend. Handed him four cans, even though in the past it has only taken three."

"Oh?" Wanda's attention piqued.

"He finished, and did a great job, mind you. Sanded them down, repainted. Nary a drop or a drip. Swept up after himself, too."

Wanda waited. It sometimes took Hazel a while to get to the point.

"Anyway. I had to go into Fort Worth to see my cardiologist. A checkup. Nothing major."

"That's good."

"Yes. So, I left him an envelope with his pay on the back stoop along with the paint cans and a stack of newspapers to use as drop cloths. When I returned, everything had a fresh coat of green paint on it, the patio was as neat as a pin, and Aaron had left."

"I see." She really didn't.

"Well, my point is, he took all the cans of paint with him. Even the empty ones."

That last tidbit of information sparked Wanda's grey cells. Had the boy used them all and tossed them in her trash can? Or did he take an almost full one away with him?

"Do you know where he lives?"

"No, but Pastor will. The Wallace family goes to our church. He recommended Aaron to me when I asked if he knew of any reliable boys who might want some extra cash in exchange for a day's work."

Good ol' observant Hazel. God bless her. "Thanks. I will check it out. You're a peach without the fuzz, as my mother used to say."

Hazel giggled. "That reminds me. I need to make an appointment at A Cut Above for a facial and to exfoliate my chin. Talk later."

Chapter Five

Wanda called Todd to let him know about her investigation so far, as she promised she would anytime she'd gleaned any information. Not only did it keep the familial ties bound, but it also fell under her duty as the neighborhood watch chairman to collaborate with the authorities.

A whoosh of air came over his phone speaker along with a honk.

"Are you on the road?"

"It's okay. I have my Bluetooth in. Whatcha got for me?"

She told him.

"Well, you work fast, Aunt Wanda."

A sense of pride swelled inside of her. She hoped he'd meant it as a compliment.

Todd continued, "Yeah, I know Aaron. Cool kid. Never had any trouble from him. A junior this year I believe."

He paused, and she heard the sound of his turn indicator click through the phone's speaker.

Okay, cancel the hearing exam.

"I can't see him doing this, Aunt Wanda, but maybe some other kids swiped the cans from him. I'll ask him about it."

Rats. She had planned to do that. Oh well, she could snoop elsewhere if someone reported anything funky at the meeting tonight. "Any word on Shari?"

"Yep. Just left the hospital and am heading back. She is in and out of semiconsciousness. She does have some brain swelling, but they are hopeful she'll make a full recovery." He paused as more highway sounds came through the phone. "And no, I am not sharing with you if she described the perp."

That last comment pierced her heart. "Todd, you've been awfully snappy to me. What have I done?"

She heard a long deep sigh come through the phone. "Okay. I'm sorry. It is just, I know how you are with these Scrabble clues. You are ready to dive off the deep end, which makes me worry about you and your close friends getting into trouble. Look what happened to Evelyn the last time."

He had a point.

"I know your heart is in the right place, Aunt Wanda, but I am a grown man, now. I appreciate your wanting to help me, but please. People are talking."

"They are?"

"I don't need you to wipe my nose anymore. I am not twelve."

The age he was when she first took him under her wing once his parents' divorce became so nasty, they both left town in shame. It seemed like yesterday, not eleven years ago. Even so, twenty-three did seem incredibly young to her. Hardly an adult . . . but then again, she'd been married by that age and had a baby.

"You are right, Todd. I apologize for any over-enthusiasm on my part. But you have to admit, this palindrome thing is a bit unnerving."

He remained silent for a minute. Wanda wondered if that meant he hadn't accepted her apology. Then his voice returned.

"Tell you what. If any more graffiti turns up in town in the form of these palindromes, then we'll see how you can help."

"Deal."

Wanda hung up, half-hoping they would show up.

Was that wrong of her?

Cheeseburger Casserole

Ingredients:

- ½ c. chopped yellow onions
- 1 lb. lean hamburger meat, cooked into crumbles
- 1 egg, well mixed
- 2 c. shredded mild cheddar cheese
- 1 can Cream of Mushroom soup - I use low sodium. Do not dilute.
- ½ tsp. garlic powder
- 1 tsp. dried green onions (chives) seasoning
- 2 c. elbow macaroni, cooked or rice

- Salt and pepper to taste, or 1 tsp. of Mrs. Dash original
- 4 strips of bacon cooked crisp and crumbled

Directions:

1. Preheat oven to 350 degrees.
2. Sauté onions in avocado or vegetable oil, and then add crumbled hamburger meat and cook on medium heat, stirring until the meat is browned all the way though. If you cook it on high it makes the meat tougher, so be patient. Drain well.
3. Turn the cooked meat into a large bowl and add the mixed egg, soup, seasonings, and cheese, reserving ½ cup of the cheese for the topping. Blend well.
4. Fold in cooked macaroni or rice.
5. Dump into a greased glass 9x12 casserole dish.
6. Sprinkle with remaining shredded cheese and bacon crumbles.
7. Bake for 30 minutes or until bubbly and cheese has melted.

Serves 4-6

For a variation, use ½ c of bottled barbeque sauce instead of the soup. Betty Sue says Fred likes it better that way. Texans do love BBQ!

Chapter Six

Later that afternoon, Priscilla phoned Wanda to let her know that Shari had awaken, though she stated her sister didn't really recall anything. Nothing more than a vague image of a person with a spray can in his or her hand before whacking her on the head with it.

"Shari crumpled and hit her head on the asphalt of the alley."

Wanda sat at her kitchen table writing this down. "Then she had two blows to the head?"

"Apparently. One in the temple and one on the side of the skull where she landed. The one in the temple, caused by the spray can, is what bled so badly. The doctors say cuts right above the eyebrows often do. She had to have stitches."

Wanda heard the quiver in her voice. Poor Priscilla. "I know this is so hard on you."

A small sob sounded through the phone. "Oh, Wanda.

It is. You have no idea. She'd only begun to turn over a new leaf. She was so excited at the chance and grateful to have Sally's and my support. We'd all begun to bond again. It's just not fair."

"But y'all will keep bonding. She needs you both even more now." And I could only hope she didn't disappoint them again. *Lord, please don't let drugs be involved.*

Priscilla blew her nose. Not in a feminine way at all. More like a goose honking through the phone.

At any other time, Wanda would be tempted to put the phone on mute and chuckle. But this was not a laughing matter. Plus, she had the impression Priscilla had much more to say. She sipped her hot tea and waited.

"The police have been grilling her about the past as if she went out there to meet some drug dealer. I got so angry I had to leave the room."

Uh, huh. Wanda knew the rollercoaster of emotions all too well. "Where are you now?"

"In the ladies."

Ah. That explained the echo. "Do you want me to drive over?"

She squeaked her response in shaky breaths. "W . . . would you? When Shari regained consciousness, I sent Betty Sue home and closed the Coffee Bean for the day. Sally had to stay at her shop, though. The lunch crowd had started plus she's got a catering job to prepare for."

Could the girl have been pulling the wool over her

sisters' eyes? Wanda set her cup in the sink and snatched up her purse. "On my way."

She'd never met Shari, but Betty Sue had and liked her immediately. Then again, Betty Sue took to everyone. Such was her nature.

As she drove up the highway, Wanda replayed the conversation in her mind.

A piece of what Priscilla had relayed didn't fit the scenario. But what?

She gripped the steering wheel harder. Think, Wanda.

Maybe skepticism had kicked in due to her own personal experiences. She'd had a time with her own daughter, Wesley. Always living life on the edge. Getting in with the wrong people. In and out of rehabs since her teens. The bumpy road of emotions and events had strained their relationship. In fact, Wanda had not heard from her in months. Guess living with the latest boyfriend, Jeremy, had been working out so far.

Conversions did happen in rehab. She knew that for a fact and secretly prayed it would one day happen for Wesley. Sometimes people had to hit rock bottom before they realized they needed the Rock of Ages. That's when they discovered that despite what their pride told them, they couldn't do it on their own strength and needed divine help, as well as the help of others.

That took a huge step that demanded trust. Addicts often found trust an extremely hard thing to grasp. They didn't trust each other, much less anyone else—especially authorities like cops, counselors, pastors, and parents. Instead, they often pushed everyone away except their supplier, including God. That is until desperation temporarily overwhelmed them.

Had that been the case for Shari?

Wanda still had not worked out the misfitting puzzle piece by the time she pulled into the parking garage. She hadn't taken but a few steps from her car when a cry arose and caught her attention.

Mary Lou Fitzgerald lifted her daughter Lucy into her arm. The toddler screwed up her face and let out another whine.

"Oh my. Fussy moment." Wanda remembered that season as though it were yesterday.

"Yes. I thought I could squeeze in a visit with Shari, but I should have known better than to try to put off naptime."

Shari's name sparked an interest. "Oh, I was heading that way, too. I didn't realize you and Shari were friends."

"Yes, we have been for a while." Lucy lurched away from her mom's shoulder. Mary Lou hoisted the wriggling child more securely in her arms. "The nurse said she can't have visitors yet." She hit a button on her fob and shoved Lucy quickly into her car seat. "I'm hoping to come back . . ."

A loud click resounded from the SUV's interior and

Mary Lou withdrew her head from the backseat. "After this one gets a long nap." She gave a wave and climbed behind the wheel.

Wanda waved back, thankful those days were long past for her. She made her way to the information desk and asked the volunteer for Shari Wright's room number anyway.

"They are moving her out of ICU to Room 349 soon. Wait here and let me contact the desk clerk to see if she can have visitors yet."

Wanda already knew the answer, so she halted the clerk with her hand. "That's all right. Actually, I am here to sit with her sister, Priscilla."

The woman hung up the receiver. "Oh, well in that case. Take the elevators to the right to the third floor, turn left, and you will find the ICU waiting room halfway down the hall. She's probably still there."

"Thanks." Wanda gave the lady a warm smile. As she walked away, she noticed the gift shop on the right. She went in, bought a packet of travel tissues, some chocolate mints, a paperback by an author she knew wrote good clean stories, and one carnation. Gifts in hand, she headed to the elevators.

As the bell dinged and the doors opened, she bumped into Todd exiting the elevator cab.

"Aunt Wanda?"

"Oh, my goodness." She pressed her hand to her heart. "You scared the bejeebers out of me."

He chuckled and took her by the elbow out of the traffic of staff and visitors coming on and off. “Here to see Priscilla?” He glanced at the carnation and gift store sack.

“How perceptive of you.” She bit her tongue, which dripped of sarcasm. Leaning against the wall, she sighed. “Sorry. Yes, I am. She phoned all in tears. I told her I’d come sit with her a while.”

He rubbed his neck. “Yeah, she got pretty ticked off at our inquiries.”

“I heard. I know you were only doing your job.”

“It wasn’t me. The county sheriff’s detectives are involved.”

A splash of cold prickles whopped Wanda in the chest. “Because?”

Todd glanced left and right then leaned into her ear. “The driver that was delayed in getting her deliveries to her. He’s missing. The van was found upturned in a ditch off a side road from Highway 67. Crates of produce scattered everywhere.”

Crates! That was the piece of the puzzle that didn’t fit.

Her brain began to whirl. “Todd. Come have a cup of coffee. There is something I need to bounce off you.”

“Okay? What about Priscilla?”

“She can wait. They are busy moving Shari out of ICU anyway from what I gather.”

Todd’s brow now resembled a commercial advertising the need for anti-wrinkle creams. With a long exhale of breath, he agreed and guided her to the café across the corridor.

They ordered two coffees and a piece of apple pie to share, and then found an empty table in the back corner. He pulled out the chair for her, then took the one across from her.

After sipping the coffee, he snagged another packet of sugar and gazed into her face. "Now, what is going on in that brain of yours?"

She leaned in so she could be heard over the din of conversations. "If the van upturned on a side road several miles away from town, then what were crates of zucchini squash, lettuce, beets, and kale doing in the alley?"

Todd slammed his spine into the wooden back of the chair. His whole expression formed a question mark.

A smirk oozed over Wanda's mouth. She couldn't help it. "Exactly. The crates were a ploy. Something tells me that palindrome is the clue to this whole mystery."

They repeated it in unison. "I did, did I?"

Her nephew shook his head. "I hate to say this, Aunt Wanda, but I think you might be right."

She smiled and sipped her coffee. About time.

His cell phone sounded. "Gotta get this."

She dismissed him from the table with a nod and watched his body language as he took the call. He slumped, turned to the wall, and rubbed his neck . . . always a bad sign.

A moment later he returned. "Sorry, gotta go."

"Todd?"

He rolled his eyes. "You may as well know. Another graffiti has turned up. This time on the alley wall of the liquor store. And yes, it's a palindrome. 'Red rum sir, is murder.'"

"Sprayed in red I imagine."

"Yep. I don't think it's from an angry customer or pious churchgoer."

Loads of Liquor, an area-wide chain, had opened last summer on Red Bud, behind the Grocery Mart. It sat across the side street from First Baptist, much to the chagrin of Pastor Paul Richardson and his elders. Historically being teetotalers, they had protested the permit, but to no avail. The City Council wanted the tax revenues.

Todd tossed their cups in the trash bin. "You coming?"

Wanda bolted from the chair so fast it toppled.

Chapter Seven

Thankfully, only the palindrome dripped red. But the fact it occurred hours later in the same alley puzzled Wanda. By the way Todd stood eying the wall scrawl, she could tell he hadn't a clue as well.

"Freshly sprayed, huh?"

Todd agreed. "Don't touch anything, okay?"

Wanda held her tongue before she spat out her thoughts. A seven-year-old who watched any CSI shows would know not to do that. Then she recalled her green fingers.

Never mind.

"When did you notice this, Mr. Garza?" Todd got out his notepad.

"When I went to take the reconciliations from the morning till to the bank at one o'clock as I do every day. It's just two blocks away, so I usually walk."

Safe enough now in Scrub Oak to carry a bank bag in

an alley, but Wanda wondered for how much longer. Crime seemed to be seeping in faster than spilled grape juice down a child's shirt. She made a mental note to talk to the neighborhood captain for district four about it. Maybe someone should be assigned to walk with Mr. Garza.

"And it was not here this morning when you opened. You're absolutely sure?"

"I would have noticed, officer. I park right over there." He pointed to a silver Honda in a designated parking spot on the other side of the dumpsters that served both Mr. Garza's liquor store and the Collin's grocery store. Collin's jeep sat next to the silver car.

Wanda took a picture of the latest brick art with her phone, then walked down the alley to the spot that held the green graffiti in order to compare handwritings. When she got there, she let out a groan. The crime tape had been removed. Only a slightly green tinted blob remained on the bricks.

Collin had already assigned someone to scrub it.

She strolled back to be in earshot of Todd and the liquor store manager. Little else in the conversation interested her. Routine stuff. No one noticed any person in the alley who shouldn't be there or appeared to be loitering. Yada yada.

She glanced at her phone—2:15. The first message had been sprayed around nine in the morning, or so she guessed since that coincided with when Shari had been assaulted and the paint had still been damp at that time. Then, several hours later another message? In a different color?

More and more it sounded like truant kids who had been interrupted in the act. But that didn't explain the crates of veggies when the delivery van never made it to the grocers. Or why Shari had not hauled them inside. Did she even have time to notice them?

A little too coincidental that it happened on her official first day as a seller. Somebody must not have wanted her to succeed in her new enterprise. But who?

"What are you so intensely pondering?"

Todd's voice made her jump. "Oh, good heavens, Todd." She pressed her hand to her chest to keep her heart from pushing out of her skin. Then she leaned against his cruiser for support.

"Sorry. Didn't mean to make you jump."

"It's all right." She swallowed. "The other graffiti down the way has been wiped off."

"I know. We told Collin we were through with the crime scene. He had our permission. Little did any of us suspect . . ." He pointed with his head to the new wording.

"True. And I want to thank you for fulfilling your promise to involve me if this occurred again."

He stood in a military at-ease stance and folded his arms. "And since it has?"

She squinted in the yellow-white glow of the afternoon sunshine. "Anyone check the dumpsters?"

"For?"

She sucked in an ounce of patience before responding. “For cans of paint, a blunt object, anything else that might be a clue?”

“The docs confirmed that a paint can probably was the weapon of choice. It would be pretty idiotic to toss it ten feet away in a public dumpster.”

She shrugged. “But in a moment of panic . . .”

He raised his hands in surrender. “Okay. Search to your heart’s content. I’ll wait here.”

“What?” He wanted her to crawl into the smelly refuge? She spun to face him head on.

Todd roared back laughing. “I’m kidding. Jimmy Bob has already had that privilege. Didn’t find anything.”

She swatted at him. “You, stinker. You had me going there.”

He kissed the air next to her cheek, still chuckling, and opened the car door for her. “Come on. I’ll take you back to the hospital so you can see Priscilla. She’s probably wondering where you are.”

“And we can talk on the way.” She scooted into the passenger seat of the police cruiser.

Todd shut the door but not before her ears picked up his mumbled comment of “if you wish” couched in a sigh.

So instead, she sat in silence all the way back.

When he let her off at the curb, she didn’t wait for him to open her door. She told him thanks and scooted out herself.

He leaned across the seat and called out to her before she had the chance to slam the car door closed. “Wait. Aunt Wanda.”

She stopped and bent down to eyeball him through the car window. “You’re double parked.”

“I’m a cop. I can.” He scrunched his forehead. “What gives?”

“Exactly what I want to know. One minute you want me involved, the next you seem to chastise me for it.” She waggled her finger at him, her tongue suddenly tied with building emotion.

He sat back and thumped the steering wheel. “You’re right. Look, you *are* a smart woman. Your insights are spot on and just between you and me I think your word clues do lead to solving crimes. But I am walking a very thin line. Not only is Chief Brooks watching my every move but now the sheriff’s detectives are as well.”

“Because?”

His exasperation spewed out with a long exhale. “Because ever since I came to town the crime has increased tenfold.”

Wanda’s heart almost stopped in mid thump. “They think you’re bringing the crime here? Why? So, you can solve it and outshine them?”

He rubbed the back of his collar. “I don’t know.”

Unless she was mistaken, his lip quivered. She wanted to draw him into a hug and kiss the boo-boo away. But her nephew was a grown man now.

"Todd, I am sorry. But you must remember crime had begun before you got here. Aurora's husband was shot two months before you came. And as for that ten-year-old murder we discovered . . ."

"True. But so far the perps were all people I knew."

Wanda noticed a shimmer in the corner of his eyes. "We all knew them. This is a small town for goodness sakes. At least it is for the moment." She opened the car door and sat down again. "Todd, why did the city council agree to add you and cadet Regan to the force?"

"The town is growing, and more people are moving in from the bigger cities." His tone flattened.

"So how can they blame you? You are under scrutiny because you are still in your first year on the force. That's protocol, right?"

"Suppose so." He nodded and crossed his arms.

"There. No need to worry, then. You're a good cop. They know it, which is why they hired you."

Color returned to his cheeks. He swallowed. "Just promise me you will stick to the shadows, Aunt Wanda, and only investigate at my directive. I don't need you playing detective behind my back. It won't look good."

"Promise. But trust is a two-way street."

He smiled. "I love you, Aunt Wanda. Never doubt that. And despite his grumbles, Chief Brooks is glad you formed the neighborhood watch." He leaned to whisper in her ear.

"Don't let him know I told you."

She chuckled. "Yo, banana boy."

He crinkled his nose. Then his eyes lit as if he'd just caught on. "A palindrome, right?"

She pinched his cheek. "Clever guy." Then she scooched out of the police car and walked into the hospital with a slightly wilted carnation and crumpled gift bag.

Wanda found Priscilla walking the halls of the third floor. When she saw Wanda, her expression brightened, and she scurried to meet her. "There you are. I worried that maybe you had a wreck."

"I'm sorry. I should have phoned to tell you I'd been delayed." Wanda handed her the gifts and then motioned for them to sit on the bench down the way near the elevator.

Priscilla raised the carnation to her nose and took a deep whiff. Then she peeked in the bag.

"Just a few things to help you pass the time while you sit with your sister."

"Thanks. That is very sweet." She gave Wanda a small hug.

"Listen, Priscilla, another graffiti message showed up earlier this afternoon."

"Really? Did they catch the guy?"

"No. Sorry. I gather Shari didn't get a good look at him."

"She says not. But everything is still fuzzy for her." Priscilla bent to glance down the hall. "I think the nurses have done their thing. Let's go."

"Wait." Wanda placed a hand on her friend's shoulder. "Please forgive me for asking, but are you sure Shari didn't know the guy?"

"Meaning?" Priscilla's eyes flashed cold. "Don't tell me you think she was back there passing drugs, too? The county police have already asked me *and her* that."

Wanda gave her the warmest smile she could muster. "No dear. But someone from her past may have tried to lure her back. It does happen. I know from experience with my Wesley."

Priscilla's face softened. "Of course, you do. I'd forgotten." She side-hugged Wanda. "Between you and me I sincerely hope not. Shari had such a terrible time the last few years. Even with visits from Sally and me. And with some of her long-time friends who continued to write to her."

Wesley had never gone to prison, but her time in the rehab center had been bad enough.

Her friend's eyebrows ruffled as she gave her forehead a brief rub. "However, it is a possibility Shari is withholding something."

"What make you say that?"

"Call it sisterly instinct." Priscilla's eyes seemed to plead for Wanda to disagree.

But how could she?

Chapter Eight

Wanda tried not to stare. The gash over Shari's right eyebrow had caused bruising around her eye in shades of purple, yellow, and green. Black stitches held it together, though swelling had set in.

She walked over to the bed and held out her hand. "Hi, Shari. I am a friend and neighbor of your sister Priscilla, and also Sally."

Priscilla let out a little gasp. "I forgot you two have never met. Shari, Wanda is a wonderful, kind friend. And she makes the world's best deviled eggs."

Shari's lips parted in a small smile. In a whispered voice she said she'd like to try them sometime.

Wanda pulled up a side chair. "Shari. I am head of the community's neighborhood watch teams. Anything you can tell me; I would appreciate it. We meet tonight, and I'd like to pass the word so we can keep an eye out." She stopped, realizing her unfortunate pun. From the expression on

Shari's swollen face, she had not gotten it, so Wanda continued. "You see, someone sprayed graffiti near to where you were assaulted and then later came back to spray some further down the alleyway."

Shari glanced at Priscilla, then back to Wanda. "Like I told the police, I came out to greet the van and ask why my order arrived so late. The guy had just set down a few of the crates and I went to inspect the produce in them."

"I see. Recall what he wore?"

She lifted one shoulder slightly from the pillows. "I dunno. Jeans, a red t-shirt. A cap. I think it had the Texas Rangers on it."

"So, no uniform?"

"No."

Wanda scooted up further in the chair. "And you are sure it was a man. What did he look like?"

"Young. My age. Dark hair, but very light skin. Almost as if he hadn't been in the sun in years."

"Tall, skinny, fat?"

Shari's gaze went to the ceiling tiles. "Average. I mean he wasn't swole."

"Huh?"

"You know. Muscular, like he worked out a lot."

Wanda's mouth made an 'o'. "Do you know why he hit you, Shari?"

Her eyes focused solely on Wanda. In a quiet voice she answered. "He didn't."

It took a moment for Shari's answer to register in Wanda's brain.

Priscilla stepped forward and took her sister's hand. "Then who did, Shari?"

Shari glanced between the two ladies. "I . . . don't . . . know. Honest. As I chewed out the driver for being so late, I heard a noise. I turned, saw a flash of a hand holding something and bam."

"Then there were two people in the alley?"

"Guess so."

Wanda squirmed. "And did you tell the police this?"

She nodded, then grimaced. The movement must have hurt her concussion.

Priscilla let go of her hand. "She needs to rest."

Wanda rose from the chair, but before she left, she bent closer. "One more thing, Shari. How many crates did you order?"

"Ten. My inventory list is on the clipboard in Collin's office."

"Thanks."

Wanda smiled at Priscilla and left the room.

Her friend's sisterly instincts were correct. Shari said a man delivered crates, they argued over the delay, then someone else knocked her out. But the real delivery van had never arrived. Wouldn't she have wondered why?

Shari Wright held something back. But what, and why?

Surely on opening day more than four crates had been

expected. Priscilla had told them half of the order had yet to arrive the evening before. Wanda needed to somehow get her hands on the inventory list. Did Collin still have it? Or the police?

She thought back to the alley scene. Four crates had been there. One with lettuce, one with kale, one of beets, one with squash varieties. If she knew how many crates were found at the scene of the turned-over truck, would they add up to what showed on Shari's inventory list?

The driver had not been found, according to Todd. Was he one of the men in the alley?

And why the palindromes?

Why return to paint another one?

"I did, did I?" "Red rum, sir, is murder." What did they mean?

Too many unresolved questions. Wanda's brain hurt.

Chapter Nine

Wanda drove back to the Grocery Mart. Not very many people were inside. The locals had done their shopping in the morning and the commuters were probably still crawling out of Fort Worth along the highway. She recalled the years her late husband had to do that day in and day out. Price to pay for a more laid-back lifestyle in a small-town atmosphere where neighbors truly knew each other.

She weaved through the aisles to the back office. The door stood ajar, but she halted when she heard voices.

"Don't ask me to do that. I won't."

Definitely Collin's voice. Wanda pretended to examine the freshness of the bakery's French loaf as she leaned a bit closer.

"She's a new-hire and already has caused trouble." Another man's voice answered back, younger sounding. Wanda didn't recognize whose.

"Hearsay is not a reason to fire someone."

"But . . ."

"I appreciate you passing on what you overheard but I'm warning you. Do not discuss this with anyone else. I'll handle this as I see fit."

A chair screeched and she heard footsteps coming to the door. Wanda eased backward a few steps and picked up a package of cinnamon rolls to examine.

Collin appeared with a twenty-something guy, one of Mr. Garza's sons. Miguel, if she recalled correctly. He appeared the same age as Isaac, Collin's son.

Interesting.

The young man shuffled back to the storeroom. Then Collin noticed Wanda. "Hi, there. Looking for some goodies for the neighborhood watch meeting? I could give you a deal on some day-old cookies."

"That would be wonderful." Wanda set the cinnamon rolls down. "May I speak with you a moment? It is about this morning."

What appeared as an objection formed on his lips, but then he nodded. "Right, you were here when it happened weren't you? Nasty business."

"Um, yes." She glanced at his open door to indicate this conversation would be better if they had it away from the curious ears of other shoppers.

He jolted a bit. "Oh, yes. Of course. Please." He motioned her inside and gestured for her to have a seat in one of the two plastic, slatted chairs in front of his desk. She recalled seeing them on special stacked outside at the end of the summer. Guess they didn't all sell. Wanda eased into one and found it quite sturdy.

He rounded the desk, returned to his own executive office chair, and leaned back. "Now, what can I do for you?"

"I have a quandary. Well, actually more than one, but . . ." Wanda hesitated a moment then decided the best thing to do was to get to the point. Collin always seemed to be an upfront sort of man. She repositioned in the seat.

"I'll be brief because I know you are a busy man."

His facial expression eased. "Thank you."

"The police tell me the van scheduled to deliver Shari's produce never arrived."

He leaned forward. "What?"

"They found it overturned in a ditch. No sign of the driver."

"Then how?"

"Exactly my question. There were four crates of produce in the alleyway near to where Shari slumped over. Where are they now?"

"In the storeroom area. We dumped the produce. It didn't seem right to sell it under the circumstances."

"Did the police dust them for fingerprints?"

"Yes, which is another reason I decided to toss the vegetables. I guess we could have washed them off and none would be the wiser, still . . ." He screwed up his lips in disgust.

Wanda gave him a few quick head bobs. Collin had always been an honest businessman with integrity. "Did they find any?"

"Fingerprints? Don't think so. I recall Chief Brooks saying if they did, all of my employees on duty at the time, me included, would have to be fingerprinted for elimination purposes. That didn't happen."

"I see. The thing is, how did those crates get there if the van never showed?"

Collin rubbed his hands down his face. "Good question. Isaac had already logged in my deliveries by then. Nothing should have been in the alley. Let me check with him. He oversees the stocking. And I'll check with Miguel who oversees the produce."

The one who seemed to not like Shari, if she had been the one they had been discussing. The fact that he oversaw the produce would give ample reasoning for his dislike. Jealousy that she was being put in charge, as it were, of this special project could be the cause.

Collin rose and went in search of his managers.

Wanda waited. She scanned the small office which smelled a tad unusual. She detected a blend of bleach, fruit, and cardboard. When she heard some thuds through the wall, she gathered that must be coming from the stock room. Of course, it was. She recalled the restrooms being in there.

A few minutes later, Collin returned with his tall, blond-haired son, Isaac. He appeared young enough to be in college due his baby face, though Wanda knew him to be in his mid-twenties, like Todd. Great guy. He worked in the family store since his teens, and he always greeted her with a handsome smile. Though now the stock manager with more responsibility, Isaac often volunteered at the food bank, and she believed he had moved into his own place in the Lake View Apartments where Todd lived.

"Hi, Mrs. Warner." His smile dazzled, as always.

"Miguel is busy with a customer." Collin stood sideways between them, his hands clasped in back.

Isaac glanced as if to get the go-ahead from Collin and then proceeded. "I understand you had a question about those crates of veggies?"

"I did. Several, actually. Do you know how many Shari expected and of what?"

"Um, I can check." He flipped through his clipboard. "Ah, ten crates. One with zucchini squash and spaghetti squash, one with beets, one kale, one Boston leaf lettuce, one of carrots, one cucumber, one with cilantro, basil, and oregano, and one with parsley, radishes, and parsnips. Then . . ." he flipped the page. "One with cabbage, purple and green, one holding broccoli and baby leaf lettuces with roots."

"And only four crates arrived. Right?"

"Yes, ma'am. Kale, the squashes, beets, and the Boston lettuce. But we pitched those out. They had fingerprint dust all over them, and, um . . . a few splatters of blood." His pale skin whitened even more as he cringed.

Wanda felt her stomach flop. "I see. But you never saw the van that brought them?"

"No, Shari insisted on inspecting them first, then she'd said she would call me or Miguel to help her stock them. I think she felt extra nervous, this being her opening day. Plus, it was almost two hours late."

Collin interrupted. "We already had stocked some organic fruits and vegetables last night, so she didn't need to order those. Also, some organic frozen meals. The orders for dry good, nuts, beans, rice, were to come in tomorrow."

"Were?" Wanda glanced at each man.

"We've cancelled those. The organic section will not officially open until Shari is well enough to return, then we will regroup." Collin perched on the edge of his desk. "Why do you want to know all of this?"

"I am helping Todd. If the real delivery van was upturned outside of town, we wondered why another one delivered only a partial order."

"Actually, we don't know it was a van. It could have been a diesel truck." Collin pushed off from the desk. "I was up front with a cashier at the time. By the time I rushed to the back after hearing the scream coming from the stock area, the vehicle had zipped away. I only saw the edge of a red taillight as it went around the corner."

Isaac cleared his throat as if signaling he wanted to speak. "Maybe that is all that was intact? The four crates, I mean. If the van had a wreck and flipped . . ." He shrugged. "They probably called in another van and delivered what they could. It would explain the time lapse."

Wanda hadn't thought of that. It made sense. The driver was nowhere to be found because he got another van or maybe a pickup truck and went to deliver what he could salvage from the wreck. If she could determine if six crates had spilled that would solve the dilemma. Now to find out the driver's name and question him, or her. But surely the county boys had already done that.

Had they sent that report to the Scrub Oak PD yet? She got up to leave, then stopped. "One more thing if you don't mind. Isaac, do you know of anyone who might want to graffiti the alleyway? A disgruntled employee or customer?"

"No ma'am."

"Did you scrub the wall?"

He glanced at his father. "Um, yeah. Miguel and I did."

She switched her attention to Collin. "Can I borrow Isaac for a moment. I want him to look at the new graffiti by Mr. Garza's shop and see if he thinks the handwriting is similar to what he scrubbed off."

Collin agreed and the two headed down the alley.

"Isaac. Miguel is Mr. Garza's son, correct?"

"Yes, why?"

"No reason. Just trying to place him."

From the eavesdropping earlier, clearly Miguel had a

grudge against a new hire, probably Shari. Wanda didn't recall any other new face in the store. But why? Wanda made a mental note to corner him when they got back, and to glance at his hands. Not that a slight green tinge would mean much, come to think of it.

Miguel could say it came from scrubbing the wall. Convenient. However, why would he return and graffiti his own father's shop? Something still didn't add up. But what?

She peeked at Isaac's hands. No color on them other than his own pale, pink skin.

They stopped in front of the red scrawl. Isaac peered at it for a moment. "Can't be one hundred percent sure, but I got a pretty good look at the other as I scrubbed it. No way the same person wrote both."

The way he blinked made Wanda wonder if he knew who wrote the second one but didn't want to divulge it for some reason. Did he cover for Shari or Miguel?

Only one way to find out. She needed to get Miguel to write a note for her. Especially one that would use the *d* that ended up in both messages. She'd figure out how to coax that out of him later. To return to the grocers now might cause suspicion anyway.

As they turned to leave, she halted. "You go on back, Isaac. And thank you. My car is around the other way."

He waved.

After he slipped back inside the grocers, she walked over to the dumpster. She held her nose as she gazed inside.

Green cloths and sponges lay inside plastic grocery sacks. Obviously from the clean-up job. But underneath, if she wasn't mistaken, lay a partially concealed can of red spray paint. As if the sacks had been purposely placed on top to hide it. Had Miguel done that? She took a picture with her phone and texted it to Todd.

Wanda then phoned to make sure he got it and told him about her visit to the Grocery Mart, and about both Miguel and Isaac.

"I know Isaac and Miguel. They hung out in high school, though I don't think Collin and his wife approved. I'm not sure if it was because Mr. Garza sells booze or something more. Anyway, I've never heard of Miguel getting into trouble, and I don't see them together except at work at this point."

"Well, it seems strange that the sacks of rags and sponges used to clean the first graffiti would be laid almost on top the can that sprayed the second one. And from the conversation I couldn't help but overhear, Miguel didn't like Shari being there at the Grocery Mart."

"Aunt Wanda, I'll go retrieve that can and bag it. See if there are any retrievable prints. But would you mind telling me why you were asking questions at the grocer's anyway?"

She felt his irritation through the phone receiver. "The crates. Why did just four show up?"

"Because the others lay in the bar ditch. Unsalvageable from the photos I saw."

"You saw them?" Her voice squeaked. "Do you have the pictures?"

"Back at the station in the file . . ."

Her pulse quickened. "Can you go check to see if you can count six crates in the wreck?"

"Aunt Wanda. I'm on patrol."

"So? That doesn't mean you have to sit in your car all night."

Silence.

Wanda lifted her cell phone from her ear to make sure they had not disconnected. Nope.

His voice finally came over the speaker. "Okay, if you do me a favor."

"Sure. What?"

"Go home. Have some supper."

"In other words, stay out of your business."

"Bingo. I promise to let you know if anything turns up."

"Okay, I'll go home, but I do have the captains' meeting tonight. I have your permission to talk about this with them?"

"Sure. But only the facts, not your suspicions."

"Agreed. But Todd?" She swallowed to wet her throat. "Something tells me Miguel knows more about this whole thing than he is letting on."

"That something being your gut instinct?" She heard his radio sound in his car. "Gotta go. One of your neighborhood watchers just reported someone spray painting a message on the side of the Vet's. Guess you want to be there, huh?"

"Naturally."

So much for going home to eat before the meeting. Wanda got out of her car and jogged the long block to the veterinary office.

There a new message lay in almost stick letters, similar to the red message at the liquor store, except in blue this time. "Name now one man."

If only she could.

Chapter Ten

Wanda tossed and turned that night. She dreamt she walked down dark alleys. At every turn, shadowy figures leaped out with spray cans to attack her. They sprayed the alphabet on her from head to toe as eerie laughter echoed in the distance. She woke in a sweat, glad to see her pjs were not marked up with words.

If she ever needed to go to church and hear a positive message, it was today. She scurried to get ready for Pastor Bob's Tuesday morning prayer service before the ladies' Bible study. Bless the pastor's heart. He delivered a great homily. After the Bible study, she caught up with Betty Sue. "Can you come for lunch later? I'll make chicken salad in avocado halves."

"Sounds good."

After they'd eaten, Wanda wrote the three palindromes out on note cards and slapped them on her kitchen table. "What do you think?"

Betty Sue took a sip of her coffee as her brow furrowed. "The last one kinda reminds me of Abraham pleading for Sodom and Gomorrah, but I doubt the artist meant it to be that."

"Artist?" Wanda scoffed. "More like vandal."

"Now, Wanda. In many cities they proudly display their wall art in the downtown areas. Like Deep Ellum in Dallas."

"Those are purposely designed and take weeks to make, I recall reading about them. These were hastily sprayed." She mimed the action in the air then sat down with a huff. "Frankly, I prefer my art to be on canvases hanging in a gallery."

"Fussbudget." Betty Sue winked. "Unlike the notes we found on our cars several months ago, we can decipher which of these messages came first. That may save valuable time."

"True. But the question remains, are they related to Shari's attack?"

"Is what related?" Evelyn, Wanda's next-door neighbor and mystery buff stood at her stoop, hand on the doorknob and peering inside. "Can I come join the fun?"

"My heavens. I didn't hear you knock." Wanda placed her hand to her heart.

"Since when do I knock?" Evelyn chuckled and sat down. "What have we got here? Another mystery?"

"You could say that. I gather you heard about Shari."

Wanda pointed to her plate as if to ask if Evelyn wanted some of it.

She declined. "I did hear. How is she?"

Betty Sue scooted over to allow room at the small kitchen table. "I spoke with Priscilla this morning. She is fine, awake, and expected to be discharged later today."

"No kidding?" Wanda felt a sense of urgency. "I wonder when we can see her?"

"You mean probe her?" Betty Sue arched one eyebrow in a teacher scowl. "Really, Wanda." The look made Wanda shudder a tad bit inside. Memories of being caught shooting a spit wad at Eddie Jenkins in third grade flashed in her head. Why had she ever thought him to be cute? Didn't he get into trouble later and drop out?

She blinked the fleeting recollection away. "You're the one who brought up the idea that the graffiti may not even be related, Betty Sue."

Her life-long friend took another sip of her coffee and then stared into the cup. Wanda hated when they quibbled. After fifty plus years of friendship they had been through a lot from being in each other's weddings to organizing baby showers prior to their kids' births and the casserole patrols after the deaths of their husbands.

"Sorry. I didn't mean to snap at you."

"No problem." Betty Sue smiled. "You are becoming quite the investigator. I'm proud of you."

Fences mended. Wanda returned to the table and

motioned with her head to Evelyn. “Fresh eyes. Do you see anything?”

“Other than they are all pali . . . what’s the word?”

“Palindromes.” The other two answered at the same time.

“And they are in order? You’re sure this time? Because the last time clues appeared around town, we didn’t know when they had been placed.”

“Yes. I saw them fairly quickly after they were sprayed.”

“Then we are assuming there is a reason they were created in this sequence? Should we Scrabble them?”

Wanda glanced at the game on top of her fridge. “I’m not sure it would help this time. Though we were playing the game right before we went to see Shari’s new organic section.”

“I did, did I? Red rum, sir is murder. Name now one man. Hmm.” Evelyn tapped her fingernail.

“The second one was on the wall of the liquor store.” Betty Sue pointed to the middle note card.

“Well, that make sense.” Evelyn gazed at them a moment more. “So, other than vandalizing walls, what’s the crime?”

Wanda swallowed the last of her iced tea from lunch. “Shari was assaulted at the time the first one was created, and the whack mark on her head resembled a spray can’s edge.”

The two relayed the rest of the information to Evelyn, including the toppled van and the mystery crates.

"So, did you find out how many crates were on the van?"

Wanda slapped her forehead. "Todd texted me last night. I fell asleep in my recliner reading but I vaguely recall his chime." She dashed into the living room to retrieve her phone. She swiped the screen.

Six crates accounted for.

"Which means four were missing. And four of them ended up in the alley. Shari heard the van. They had to be in the van."

Evelyn rubbed her hand down her chin. "Did anyone else hear the van?"

Betty Sue leaned forward. "What are you thinking?"

"Simply that if no one else heard it, maybe Shari didn't. She just said she did."

Wanda sat back down. "Why?"

Evelyn shrugged.

Wanda shook her head. "Collin told me he saw the taillights as it rounded the corner and left. So, there was a delivery."

Evelyn lifted a finger. "Or anyone else. Lots of people use it as a short cut instead of going down Main."

"It could be she simply interrupted the graffiti artist who then bonked her on the head and ran off." Betty Sue glanced at each of her friends to weight their response.

"Unless she saw the delivery wasn't what she expected and asked too many questions, so the perp picked up the can left by the artist, who ran at the sound of a vehicle coming down the alley, and whacked her with it, then split." Evelyn pantomimed the scene as she spoke.

Wanda sat back. "Right. Shari mentioned something about two people in the alley. The graffiti may be a red herring. Wrong place wrong time. Then the artist returns to leave his or her cryptic messages later in the day as planned."

The three women glanced at each other and rejected that theory with a mutual head shake.

"What then?" Wanda let out and exasperated sigh.

The other two pondered that question and remained silent. The kitchen clock ticked. The coffee brewer let off a hiss and Sophie snorted as she turned in her sleep, snug in her basket by the fridge.

An idea zipped into Wanda's brain, disturbing the peace. She stood with a jolt. "Or she knew the perp, realizing he was not the driver she expected, and he tried to silence her. In that case, she made up the story about the second guy."

"Why?" Betty Sue and Evelyn asked in unison.

"That is exactly what we have to find out. Let's go."

She grabbed her purse, stopped at the stoop, and twisted back around to her friends. "You two coming?"

"Where?" Betty Sue stood and pushed in her chair.

Evelyn did the same.

"I'll tell you on the way." Wanda motioned them out the backdoor.

Chapter Eleven

"I need to speak with Collin." Wanda spoke into her phone clipped to the handle perched in the cup holder.

A young voice answered. "He's not here. Can I take a message?"

"How about Isaac?"

The worker told her to hold. In a moment she heard him pick up the receiver. "Grocery Mart, Isaac speaking. How can I help you?"

"Isaac. Mrs. Warner. What is the name of the delivery company that brought Shari's organic order?"

"Organic Options. They only deliver for local organic growers in Johnson, Tarrant, and Parker counties. Why?"

In the rearview mirror, Wanda noticed Evelyn in the back seat grab a pen and notepad from her purse to jot the information down. She gave her a thumbs up gesture. "Just wondering. I didn't realize organic farming had caught on in North Texas."

"Yes, ma'am. There are quite a few. Fifteen or more. Shari spent weeks visiting each one, recording in her laptop what they offered, tasting their products. After some discussion, she and Dad chose the ones they liked and then contracted Organic Options to be the delivery service."

"Ah, so her produce came from different locations?"

"I think so. But why . . ."

"Just curious. Thanks. Bye."

She disconnected quickly to avoid hedging any more of the young man's queries.

"What are you thinking?" Betty Sue twisted in the passenger seat to face Wanda.

"I have a feeling that one of those farms may have been delivering more than produce."

"Wanda." Betty Sue slapped her arm. "Shari got clean in rehab."

"I know. But what if Evelyn is correct? Shari recognized the driver from when she wasn't clean?"

"And he silenced her." Evelyn bobbed her head and wrote that on her notepad.

Betty Sue shook her curls and scooted back to face the windshield. "It doesn't fit. Why would he be in the alley?"

Wanda craned her neck to view in her sideview mirror as she turned the corner to head up Woodway. "Todd said the six crates were accounted for at the scene of the wreck. So, the van that showed up with four crates was a decoy. There must be a reason. My guess is the owner of the mystery van caused the wreck in the first place."

"And then pretended to be from Organic Options. But Shari noticed something seemed wrong and paid the penalty?"

"We'll find out." She punched in the gate code that opened into the Lake View Apartments. "It's a little after two o'clock. Todd might be awake before starting his evening shift."

Betty Sue groaned. "You know this is not going to turn out well, right?"

Wanda flashed her an innocent expression as she batted her eyelashes. "Whatever do you mean?"

Evelyn clucked her tongue and stared out the side window. "She brought us along to diffuse his reaction. When are we ever gonna learn, Betty Sue?"

Wanda pulled up to Building Four. "You ladies coming?"

Evelyn unclicked her seat belt and tapped Betty Sue on the shoulder. "Guess we better join her. I can't stand the sight of blood, except on TV."

Betty Sue giggled as she climbed out of the passenger seat.

The three strolled up the walkway to apartment 408.

"Perhaps you should text him first." Betty Sue pointed to Wanda's purse.

"Drat, I left the phone in the console." Wanda rubbed her forehead. "Why am I so forgetful these days. Oh, well."

She knocked on the door in a rhythm he'd recognize as hers.

A thudding of bare feet could be heard before the door opened a crack and a disheveled-haired nephew poked his head out. He squinted and then let out a growl. "Aunt Wanda. You brought your friends?"

"We've been brainstorming."

"Right. Just a minute." He closed the door.

More like four minutes later it reopened, and he motioned them inside. The aroma of freshly sprayed ocean breeze air freshener almost gagged Wanda. She swallowed to keep from coughing. Better than his smelly sock odor the last time she came.

He shoved some papers to the floor and offered the sofa. Then he sat across from the three ladies in an easy chair. "Well?"

Wanda rose. "Evelyn, you explain. I'll make coffee."

Her friend's mouth could have caught a fly. Wanda smiled as sweetly as she could and walked into the kitchen.

Todd chuckled. "She got ya that time. So, spill, Evelyn."

With Betty Sue's occasional insertions, Evelyn proceeded to tell him of their conversation around Wanda's kitchen table and then in the car on the way over there. When she had finished, Wanda reappeared with four cups of coffee, sugar, and cream. "He doesn't buy Stevia."

Todd stuck out his tongue. "Nasty aftertaste."

Betty Sue shrugged, dropped a teaspoon of sugar into

her brew and stirred.

"So, Todd. Whatcha think? Perhaps the graffiti and Shari's assault may not be related at all."

He took his sweet time sipping his coffee before responding.

Wanda began to jiggle her knee. Was this Todd's attempt to get back at her for banging on his door and bringing unannounced guests?

Evelyn stared at the ceiling and Betty Sue chewed her lip as her cheeks turned rosy, a sure sign she stifled a laugh. They all knew waiting was not one of Wanda's best skills.

Wanda eyed each of them and steadied her breath. She'd show them. She nonchalantly sat back and pulled on her pant leg as she waited. Then she realized her nephew's brain wheels might actually be spinning. His eyes narrowed, and he stared off to the side.

"I get what you are saying. The graffiti might be a diversion. I mean the last two. Chief phoned me about ten minutes before you arrived. Forensics think the last two are in the same handwriting but not the same as the first one. Although they think they were all written by someone in their mid-twenties, or early thirties at the most."

Todd's age. Which meant he likely knew the culprits, maybe even went to school with them back in the day.

Oh, brother.

Chapter Twelve

"You're saying the only one that may be relevant to Shari's assault is 'I did, did I?'" Wanda felt her pulse rate rise.

Todd raised his hands in surrender. "I'm not saying anything. Look, I agree. The fact that four crates were delivered, matching part of Shari's order, is significant considering the rest on the invoice can be accounted for at the wreck site."

"Why? It makes sense they would deliver what they could." Evelyn leaned forward.

"Their dispatch didn't send anyone else." Todd tilted his head as if to make his point.

Evelyn straightened. "Can forensics determine what type of van came, then?"

"No, it hasn't rained in quite a while so no viable tire treads were gleaned from the alleyway, and besides trucks and vans pass through all the time, so there's no telling which were which."

"And Shari hasn't been able to describe the van or the driver?"

"Nope. She says it all happened too quickly."

Wanda scoffed, so all eyes turned toward her. "She told us she believed there were two people in the alley. You don't believe that, dear nephew, do you? I can tell by the look in your eye."

"I don't, Aunt Wanda. Last evening, I re-enacted the scene with two of the clerks and Priscilla. Shari, according to Priscilla, heard the van's engines and went to meet it. She left the back door open so they could haul in the produce. A good two or three minutes passed before Priscilla heard Shari scream. Priscilla recalls then hearing the van's tires screeching as it left the alley but by the time she weaved through the aisles to the back delivery area, it had disappeared."

"Giving Shari ample opportunity to speak to the driver before she got whacked. Which means she may have figured out something she wasn't supposed to." Wanda sat back and crossed her arms.

Betty Sue's expression sank. "Or they silenced her because she chickened out at the last minute."

Wanda knew she'd been rooting for Shari to turn over this new leaf and be a success. Wanda didn't blame her. She'd been on that roller coaster ride with her own daughter, filled with the same hope, only to get off it a skeptic.

"Could be either scenario or one we haven't figured out yet. Now that she is back in her apartment, I am to interview her again this afternoon, so now is as good a time as any." He swiveled to face Betty Sue. "Would you come along? She knows you and knows you have her best interest at heart. It might help."

Betty Sue glanced at Wanda as if asking permission. Wanda swallowed her jealousy twinge and agreed. "He's right, Betty Sue. She might open up to you. Especially if Priscilla or Sally aren't present. I imagine one of them is hovering over her now, so Evelyn and I could distract them if you like, Todd."

"Good insight. If it were Wesley, I would be." He paused. "Sorry, Aunt Wanda, you know what I mean."

She did. While he lived with her during his awkward teen years, Wesley had returned home in one of her prodigal moments and the two years they spent together under Wanda's roof had further bonded them even though they were six years apart in age. Until Wesley once again fell from grace. Todd had been a junior in high school by then, Wesley still struggling as a sophomore at an area community college. It had devastated him but, perhaps in a weird way, led him down the path to law enforcement so he could help others not get sucked into that world. An example of how God can turn evil into good.

Wanda gathered the mugs and put them in his dishwasher, pretending not to notice the dirty dishes he'd shoved inside the oven, out of sight but visible through the glass window in the door. So that's what he'd been doing as she and her friends waited on his doorstep. She chuckled and shook her head before joining the others.

They trotted single file down the walkway to building five and up the stairs to 524. Todd tapped the knocker on the door. Sally answered.

"Hi Sally." He held out his badge. "I am here on official business. I need to speak with Shari. My aunt and her friends are here on a social call. We happened to meet up on the way. May we come in?"

Sally hesitated and looked behind her. Then one shoulder lifted. "Sure, I guess." She opened the door all the way for the four of them to traipse into the living room. "Shari is in the bedroom. But she is dressed. This way."

Todd followed her down the small hallway that separated the bathroom and the bedroom from the living area. Wanda motioned for Betty Sue to go along, too.

She and Evelyn waited in the living room. When Sally came out, Wanda explained. "We don't want to crowd her, and Betty Sue knows her best. We came to see about you."

"Ah." Sally blinked, probably realizing she should play hostess, and asked them to be seated. "Can I get you ladies anything. I am not sure what Shari has, but . . ."

"No, thanks. We just had a cup of coffee." Wanda smoothed the seam of her pants. "How is she doing?"

"Oh, she's still weak. Fierce headache, but she's in

good spirits. Even had a visit from an old friend from high school."

"How nice."

Sally nodded. "It has been a hard time for her, but a couple of true-blues stood by her, writing to her almost as much as Priscilla and I did."

Evelyn perched on the edge of the sofa. "Good friends like that are hard to find. I'm glad she has them."

An awkward silence settled for a moment. Wanda struggled for the next topic to keep Sally talking. "What is the doctor telling you?"

"Oh, he said we are to stay with her the next forty-eight hours to be sure she doesn't fall or show signs of confusion and such." She shook her head. "She has that nasty gash, you know."

"I see. Wise." Wanda tried to listen to Sally with one ear and the voices down the hall with the other but those were too muted. "Though I know it is hard on both you and Priscilla with establishments to run."

The three spent the next fifteen minutes in awkward conversation snippets mostly about Sally's Salad Bar and about upcoming town events. Then they heard the door creak. Todd appeared with Betty Sue.

Betty Sue smiled. "You two can go in but she is very tired. Don't visit too long. Todd, let's wait outside. It is a mild day and I need fresh air in these old lungs."

Sally stood, her face showing relief that she didn't have

to play hostess too much longer.

Wanda made her way to Shari's room with Evelyn following behind her. "Hi, Shari. We won't stay long. I only wanted to ask what you like to eat. Several of the ladies at the church will jump at the chance to cook but I didn't know if you ate meat, or . . ." she stopped. What do those heavy into organics eat?

"I do eat meat, mostly chicken. I prefer them to be free range chickens or grass-fed beef, though. Collin is stocking both now. And I love all veggies. Especially raw since I have a juicer. And rice. Brown or wild grain. I am not that fond of anything sweet."

Wanda mentally wrote this down. "Great I will pass on the word. Good to see you out of the hospital. Must have been a scary thing for you."

She nodded then flinched as if moving her head still caused her pain.

"By any chance, did you . . ."

Evelyn grabbed her elbow before Wanda could begin to interrogate. Wanda turned and saw the "no, don't" in her eyes. "Never mind. You look a bit pale. Get rest."

Shari's lips moved into a semi smile, and she closed her eyes.

Wanda and Evelyn left the room and returned to the living room, said their goodbyes, then trotted down the stairs to meet Betty Sue and Todd. By the time they reached the last step Wanda's curiosity gene was ready to burst.

"Well?"

Betty Sue's face sobered. A sadness appeared in her eyes. "She says she doesn't recall a thing. She went out the back, saw the four crates, took stock of what they had inside and then turned to ask where the rest were. She states the driver or someone else then whacked her in the head without saying a word. All went black."

"Yeah, and she claims it happened so quickly she can't give a good description of the perp. Only a generic one about jeans, red shirt, and a baseball hat."

"She's lying." Betty Sue glanced at Todd and let out a long sigh. "I can tell. I taught school way too long to not notice telltale facial expressions."

Todd scuffed his boot toe against the concrete. "My assessment exactly. Shari not only knew her assailant, but she is also covering for him."

"Or her." Wanda and Betty Sue said it at the same time.

Wanda laughed. "We really have to stop doing that."

Betty Sue's face lightened. "We know each other too well, I guess."

Todd rolled his eyes. "I've got to shower, change, and go do my report. Later, ladies."

He strolled away his hands shoved deep into his jean pockets. His shoulders slumped.

Wanda sighed. Hurt and disappointment in Wesley had surfaced all over again.

Surely nothing more, right? No. Shari would never be

Todd's type, would she? Wanda had to admit she was petite and had a cute face, but . . .

Betty Sue laced her arm through Wanda's elbow. "Don't worry. I didn't sense any sparks between them."

The lump in her throat dissolved. She patted Betty Sue's hand. "Good."

Even so, opposites did attract. And they did live in units across from each other. Todd could see her balcony from his bedroom window . . . if he wanted to, that is. But he wouldn't. He had been raised as a gentleman.

She followed her friends back to her vehicle.

Evelyn leaned against Wanda's car and looked up at a plane flying overhead as she waited for Wanda to click the fob. "If Shari is lying, then how do we discover the truth?"

Wanda glanced upward as well. A small silver speck inched across the sky. Hard to believe it traveled over 500 mph and held 200 passengers packed in like sardines headed to DFW airport. How many were coming home, how many were arriving to visit friends, and how many were preparing for a business meeting?

Wanda blinked. Too many questions floated in her head. She needed sugar. This new diet was getting to her. She refocused on Evelyn's query, which seemed the most pertinent. "We look for clues that prove she's lying. I still believe the graffiti is somehow tied to this."

"But, Wanda, Todd said the handwritings were different." Betty Sue scrunched her eyebrows, making them almost touch.

"Which means more than one person is involved. The last one told us to 'name now one man'. Perhaps when we can, then we can name the other."

"Or maybe someone is covering up their tracks to steer us in another direction." Evelyn cocked her head in a nod to emphasize her point.

"Meaning?" Wanda didn't quite see where her friend's brain led her.

"If there was more than one writer, then it would be logical to assume a teen gang had been marking and then were frightened away by a van arriving."

"I see." Betty Sue's eyes twinkled with excitement. "The perp hires or persuades someone else to leave the other two messages, so we don't think they have any relevance."

Wanda snapped her fingers. "Ah, that way we don't delve too deeply into the meaning of the first. 'I did, did I?' It is almost a taunt to find the person guilty, whoever it is."

"Yep." Evelyn pushed off. "Ready to get out of here?"

Wanda thought for a moment. "Not yet. I have a strange premonition something is about to . . ."

She twisted around to watch Todd thudding down the stairs, two at a time.

Chapter Thirteen

Todd jogged to her side and halted, slightly out of breath.

"Just got a call. Another graffiti. And this time, a witness."

"Who? Where?"

"Behind the grocers again, Aunt Wanda. Isaac witnessed it. I'm heading there now." He dug his keys from his pocket. She noticed his badge clipped to the loop in his jeans.

Isaac, huh? "Can we tag along?"

"I don't see why not. Just remember, you are only concerned citizen observers. Nothing more." He pointed a finger at each of their noses. "Do not touch anything or talk to anyone. Please."

Wanda grinned. "Well, since you said the magic word, okay."

His serious face cracked into a smile. "Let's go." He

began to trot to his car then turned, jogging backwards. "By the way, I can speed. You, on the other hand, better not. See ya there in a few."

Wanda waved. "Drat."

Evelyn laughed as she slid into the passenger seat.

Betty Sue climbed into the back and clicked her seat belt. "Todd knows how long it takes to get there. If you arrive any sooner, he will ticket you, you know."

Wanda shoved the key in the ignition. "I know." She backed out and drove 29 mph all the way there, growling as she did. He wanted her to show up after he'd surveyed the scene and gathered the pertinent evidence. Well, fine. She had another idea.

She wanted to take another look at the four crates. And what better time than when everyone else would be distracted out in the alley?

Chapter Fourteen

"Borrow or rob." Wanda read the scrawl out loud as she took a photo of it with her phone. She glanced at the wall one more time before turning her focus to Isaac, who spoke with Todd. His body had relaxed a bit. The adrenaline of the incident must have eased, or his guilt was masked by a forced nonchalance. After all, as stock manager he oversaw everything that came in and out of that grocery. Yet he never mentioned the four crates as a partial delivery. What did he know that she didn't?

She strained to hear their conversation as she watched them.

"I brought out those flattened boxes to lean against the dumpster." He pointed toward two stacks of cardboard tied together with string. "We always do that the day before the recycle truck comes."

"As opposed to the day of?" Todd eyed him as he scribbled in his notepad.

"Yes, sir. Call it community service. They are free for

the taking and some people use them when they move. Others to store away things they don't use."

"And that's when you caught the graffiti artist in action."

Isaac bobbed his head. "He was dressed in jeans and a light gray hooded jacket."

"He? You're sure it was a man?"

"I guess, but I didn't really get a good look. I just assumed . . ."

"Never saw him at the store?"

Isaac shrugged and turned toward the sound of Jimmy Bob's cruiser bumping down the pot-holed alley.

Well, at least now she knew it was probably a male, not female. If she could believe Isaac. He'd never given her any reason to doubt his word before.

"Name now one man." Seems perhaps they could be close to doing just that.

Now to name the other. She slipped into the backdoor, left it open a crack in case it self-locked, and walked over to the crates stacked in the corner. It took a moment for her eyes to adjust to the dimly lit room. How did they ever read labels in here?

Well, the local police made it easy to determine which ones were involved in the attack on Shari. Traces of fingerprint powder still blackened the edges of four of them placed off to the side by themselves. She pulled out her cell phone. Turning on the flashlight app, she scanned the outsides of each one.

Bingo. A small, fluffy gray thread appeared on one of the crate staples. Most likely from a sleeve. Assuming the person who carried the crate was the same person who unloaded them, the sharp edge must have snagged their clothes.

She raised her hands to her sides and mimed herself lifting and carrying a crate. Most likely the snag would be on the left sleeve.

"What are you doing?"

Wanda turned to see Todd's silhouette in the doorway.

"You wanted me to stay out of your way, so I . . ."

"Decide to snoop in here. Why?" He strolled toward her, his boots thunking on the concrete floor.

"To see if I could find any evidence of who carried these crates." She held up the string pinched between two fingers. "Such as this."

"What do you have there?" He walked closer. She smelled men's shampoo as he bent to eye her find. So, he had been in the shower when the phone rang. She'd thought his buzzed head looked damp. She wished he'd grow his hair out a bit, the slight wave in his locks made him so much more handsome. Maybe then, a nice girl would notice him.

She placed the fuzzy evidence in his hand. "Light gray I believe. Mostly likely from a fleece hooded jacket?"

He took a bag from his back pocket and placed the string inside. "Could have been there for months. Who knows how many people have handled this crate? Or it could have been from an employee here assigned to stack them."

"Spoiled sport." She pretended to pout, though she knew his surmise could be correct.

"I'll have forensics give it a once over anyway."

"And perhaps take a glance at the sleeve of the person who painted this latest message to see if there is a snag about here?" She pointed to her arm. "I heard Isaac give you the description."

"I figured you did." Then his eyes became rounder. "Ah, so that was what you were doing when I came in here. Acting out how to carry the crate and where the snag would be."

"Guilty." She tried oh so hard not to be smug.

"There is something else, too." She motioned him to draw nearer to the four crates. "The label on this one reads Macon, GA. Shari told Priscilla she only bought from local farmers. This came from out of state."

Todd raised up. "Which means it couldn't be one of the original crates. We knew six were accounted for in the accident, but there still lay the possibility the van carried more than one order. Now, it appears these crates were decoys."

Wanda nodded and turned the flashlight app back on. "Forensics used black fingerprint powder. Correct?" She aimed the beam to the edge of the crate where some dark granules remained.

"Correct." Todd crouched down.

"So, what is this white powder?" She moved the light to the back left corner.

She heard Todd suck in a breath as he stood.

"It's coke, right?"

"Looks like it. One way to find out." He got out his phone and punched the second button. "Jimmy Bob. Call County forensics. Get them over here now." He hung up and clicked his tongue. "How could they miss this?"

Wanda figured the question was a rhetorical one. She bit her lip.

Todd shook his head. "Aunt Wanda, maybe we do need to put you on the force."

She folded her arms. "Nah, think I'll hang up my shingle as a consultant. I'd make more money."

Her nephew's laugh echoed throughout the storeroom.

But Wanda didn't join in the joviality. Odds were the substance was illegal. Crack, heroin, flakka. Whatever the compound, it wasn't baby powder. That meant drugs were being smuggled in the produce and someone at the Grocery Mart may be involved.

Shari described the driver as wearing jeans, a red tee, and a cap, and her assailant with a light gray sleeve. If they could believe she saw two. Isaac described a someone with a hooded jacket that might be a match. But lots of younger folk wore light gray fleece these days.

Deep inside she wanted to believe Shari wasn't involved, but experience told her otherwise. Drug addiction was supported by the money earned in distribution. The two went hand in hand. One needed money to buy the stuff and sell it to those who needed it. Way too often the seller had become hooked as well and had already spent all of their income on their habit.

"Borrow or rob." If a person borrowed too much of what they were to sell, the drug lord goons would track them down. If they robbed to earn the money to support their habit, the police would be on their trail. Either way spelled trouble.

Temptation would always be lurking around the corner, waiting for the next victim to slip up. The devil was like a prowling lion waiting to devour if she recalled Peter's epistle correctly. Her heart ached for Sally and Priscilla.

Blinking back a tear, Wanda left the evidence in the hands of the experts. She had other duties. As a friend, to be there for those who tried to believe a person hooked into this mess could change. As the head of the neighborhood watch, she had the duty to report the possibility of a drug ring in town. The captains needed to be told. She'd have to call a special meeting tonight.

Wanda's face must have shown her concern because Betty Sue rushed to meet her. "I wondered where you had gone. What's wrong?"

She pulled her to the side and motioned for Evelyn to

join them.

"What's up?" Evelyn placed her hands to her hips. "Why the long face?"

"I decided to have one more peek at the four crates. When I did, I found white powder in the corner of one of them. Todd thinks it is drugs. He is calling in the county guys."

Betty Sue gasped.

"Wait a minute." Evelyn shook her head. "How do you know it was one of those crates?"

"Fingerprint dust on the outside of them."

"Oh, dear." Betty Sue's eyes shimmered. "Do you think Shari is involved?"

Wanda shrugged. "Well, we all suspect she is either lying or withholding the truth. I can see two circumstances. One, she knew about the drug smuggling and was in on it. The organic produce is really a front. She sees not all of the amount to be delivered is there, fights with the van driver thinking he is holding out on her, and he whacks her then sprays the message to incriminate her."

"Where would he get the paint?"

"From the alley. Didn't you notice the advertisements in the Grocery Mart window? They are stenciled in green paint. My guess is the employees were making the posters and left a can lying around."

Betty Sue waggled her head as if considering it. "And the other scenario?"

"Might be that she saw the drugs when she examined the crates, confronted the driver, who then panicked and whacked her. Then to clear himself, he scrawls the message and puts the blame on her."

Evelyn placed a hand on her shoulder. "Brilliant my dear Watson. Both fit."

"Does Todd know this?" Betty Sue stepped closer.

"I forgot to mention it to him."

"Forgot to mention what?" The women jumped at the sound of a familiar male voice.

"Todd." Wanda faked a half-swoon. "Never sneak up on an old lady like that. Our tickers are not as strong as yours."

He chuckled. "Aunt Wanda, I suspect you will outlive me. Now what did you forget to mention?"

When she told him, his cheeks reddened. Yes, he should have noticed the posters and put it together. She almost hated to one-up him. Almost.

He rubbed his brow. "Well, I guess I need to ask Collin why he failed to mention that fact. I'll speak with him once we determine the contents of the white powder you discovered. For now, ladies, do me a favor and keep this all to yourselves."

Wanda licked her finger and crossed her heart. Betty Sue and Evelyn only bobbed their heads firmly.

Todd winked and strolled away.

Wanda whispered to the other two ladies. "At least he

didn't say to stop investigating. If he and the county team missed the connection with the grocery ads and the peculiar white power, who knows what else they missed. Come on."

Chapter Fifteen

"Where are we going?" Betty Sue scurried to keep up with Wanda's purposeful strides as she rounded the corner to the front of the store then stopped to gaze at the window signs.

"To the hardware store. I want to know when the Grocery Mart purchased those cans and that will tell us how long the signs have been up unless you two know it. I haven't been shopping in an opossum's age. Been getting deliveries from that megastore, but don't tell Collin."

"I do that at least once a month. They have so many things he doesn't carry." Evelyn pushed her mouth to one side.

Betty Sue waggled her finger at them playfully.

"Hey, but I shopped last week, and I didn't notice them. In fact, I am sure they were not up. Other ads had been posted. I recall the raisin bran flakes were on special, so I bought two boxes. So was the half-gallon of whole milk."

Evelyn turned to Betty Sue. "Don't you start in on me."

"I wouldn't think of it. You have always maintained your trim figure. But still, whole milk does have a lot of carbs and sugars . . ."

Wanda cut her off. "Let's go to Hardware Haven then walk over to the Hook and Owl. I am so hungry. Lunch didn't stick with me."

Evelyn rubbed her hands. "Irish stew and soda bread. Definitely."

"Mmmm." Wanda wiped her tongue across her lips. "I'm in the mood for Dublin coddle." She could almost smell the traditional meal containing sausages, onions, and potatoes.

Betty Sue sighed. "Very well. I'll tag along in case either of you keel over and I need to call 9-1-1. They do make a good, stewed kale."

Wanda and Evelyn shuddered at the same time.

Then Evelyn halted in mid-step. "Wait, then we will have to walk all the way back here to get the car."

"It's a little over three blocks, Ev. Well, maybe four from the Hook and Owl, but seriously. You walk more than that in the Christmas parade every year." Betty Sue smiled.

"True. Okay, you've won me over. After slurping down a bowl or two of Irish stew it'll probably do me good." She patted her tummy and picked up her pace.

Betty Sue turned to Wanda and held up two fingers, a question on her face. Hook and Owl's bowls were huge.

Wanda stifled a laugh and kept walking.

They entered the Hardware store. Henry greeted them with his famous full-toothed grin. "Ladies. Welcome. How can I help you?"

Wanda walked to the counter. "When I was in here last and asked about the green paint, you told me about Hazel buying a few cans and Fix-it Finn but not that the Grocery Mart had bought some as well. Do you recall when?"

He slightly blushed. "It honestly didn't occur to me. They buy paint cans all the time to use on their displays. Usually, Collin orders a case each of red, green, black, and blue."

"How many are in a case?" Wanda felt she should know but couldn't think of it off the top of her head.

"Twelve." He looked in the computer. "He last ordered three weeks ago. Why?"

"Is there any way to trace the cans? I mean if we brought in one, could you tell if it was in that batch?"

Evelyn leaned in and whispered in Wanda's ear. "You're not thinking of dumpster diving, are you?"

Wanda hushed her.

Henry pondered her question. "They all have UPC coding, but I just hand-enter the price and order number in the computer. I don't track that other stuff like the large retail stores. For me it is enough to know I had twelve and sold four."

"I see. So there really is no way of knowing where the

graffiti artist, who is gracing our fair town with his talent, got his paint?"

"All I can say is I haven't had any strangers in my store in over a month."

Wanda ventured a bit further. "But you can tell me how many cans you've sold and if you sold any green or red ones to anyone other than Collin?"

"Well . . . yes. Hang on. You know Hazel bought some for Aaron to use. I have sold two blue cans to the Montgomery's. They were redoing their swing set for their grandson. Lakeview Apartments bought two cases of black to redo their railings. No wait. That wasn't spray. Ah, I sold two cans of black last week, not sure to whom, though. They paid cash."

"No red or blue?"

"Don't think so, Wanda." He scanned his ledger again. "Nope. Other than to Collin, no."

Wanda's brain jolted. *Aha.* She tapped the counter. "Henry, thank you. You have been of great help." Then she bought another box of mints and motioned to her friends for them all to exit.

Once outside, Evelyn grabbed Wanda by the sleeve. "Do you think our mural maker works at the Grocery Mart?"

"Seems that way. Though I do recall Henry saying spray paint cans last a long time and could have been purchased a year or so ago."

Betty Sue tugged her sleeve. "What if whoever is doing this bought their cans elsewhere, like those super home improvement stores in Cleburne or Burleson? Both are less than a half-hour away."

Wanda's enthusiasm drooped along with her shoulders. "Well, then. We need to find a can and take it to those stores. If the UPC codes do not match or they don't carry that brand, then we will know, won't we?"

Betty Sue raised one hand in a pledge. "I am not searching a dumpster. No way."

Evelyn shook her head back and forth. "Uh, uh. Don't look at me."

Wanda sighed. "Then I will. Though I'm fairly sure forensics already got the red can."

Evelyn huffed out a breath. "Okay, Ms. Hardhead. I'll join you. Someone has to give you a boost. Let's do it after hours though. And in grubbier clothes than these. My slacks are brand new."

"And they are very becoming on you. Not everyone can wear persimmon." Betty Sue plastered on her sweet Southern lady smile.

"Thank you. They were on sale at Bargain Boutique."

"Okay." Wanda interrupted. "But let's go early in the morning. Say six, just before dawn. I don't want my nephew patrolling and see us traipsing in the alley with flashlights tonight."

"True." Evelyn snickered. "Now let's go eat."

Chapter Sixteen

Over an early dinner the three chatted about other things. Their kids, the news, the weather, the high school band's chance of advancing to state. Not talking about crime or graffiti or palindromes or drugs lifted Wanda's spirits. The advice Paul gave the Philippians to think on the positive, noble, and true things, resonated in her soul. She silently sent up a prayer that Shari would not be involved as she chewed her savory sausage.

On the walk back to the car, she began to roll the messages around in her head again. The last one puzzled her the most. "Borrow or rob." Did the van driver only borrow the cocaine, or whatever it was? Or did he rob it from the dealers and decide to—what did they call it? —lace it with powdered milk or something. Maybe the graffiti had nothing to do with anything and it really was just a gang of hoodlums trashing their town. If so, why palindromes?

Maybe this had become a new thing with teens. Like

rap had been for so long. She made a mental note to cruise some social media sites to find out. "Why don't we all go back to my place for coffee and look over these messages again."

"Since you are driving, Wanda, it makes sense. I live next door anyway." Evelyn always seemed ready to investigate.

Betty Sue usually held back a bit, as she did this time. "I think I will pass. I'm quite tired, really. The neighbor's new dog yelped half the night."

"I'll drive you home, then. That way you won't have to walk the extra blocks."

For once the fitness queen agreed. She must be tired.

When they pulled into her driveway, Betty Sue stifled a yawn. "Good luck in the morning, you two."

Evelyn turned wide-eyed to Wanda. "Got any of that buttermilk pie left?"

"Four slices. One definitely has your name on it."

"Goodie. I have just enough room."

After two helpings of stew Wanda wondered how, especially with her perpetual concave stomach. The woman could eat a horse and not gain an ounce. "Lord, why did you make me to where smelling a piece of pie adds two pounds?"

"Excuse me?"

"Nothing." She pulled into the drive and let her friend in the backdoor. Sophie greeted her as if Wanda had been gone for at least a week.

"Pardon me while I feed her royal highness, or we will never get any peace."

Evelyn shooed the thought away. "You go ahead. I think I will check on Tweety and be back in a few." She left to care for her pet bird.

Wanda decided to make a pot of coffee, brewed with a stick of cinnamon and a few drops of vanilla extract in the grounds, instead of using the pods. The last drip gurgled when Evelyn returned. She poured them both a cup and then warmed the pie slices in the microwave. Then she got out the note cards and she wrote the latest message on a fresh one.

As they ate the pie and sipped their coffee, the two stared at the palindromes in silence. Then Wanda read them aloud.

"I did, did I?"

"Red rum sir, is murder."

"Name now one man."

"Borrow or rob."

Evelyn glanced up. "Do you have the photos of these?"

"All but the first one. I didn't think of taking it until later, but Isaac and Miguel had already scrubbed it off. You know Collin." She did an eye roll.

"Can you print them out from your phone? Seeing the originals may jiggle a brain cell or two."

Wanda snapped her fingers. "Great idea. Back in a

few."

She jogged down the hall to her guest room-slash-office and printed out the pictures on her wireless printer. Two months prior she had Todd help her move her desk in there so the computer whirs and blinky lights no longer disturbed her sleep. She rarely had guests anyway unless one of the kids came to visit. The third bedroom she kept for Wesley, just in case. She sighed as she passed it.

Then she paddled back with the prints and laid them on the kitchen table. "Well?"

Evelyn eyed them one at a time and then the note cards again.

"Hmm. I agree. The second and third one appear to be scrawled—is that the right word?—by the same hand. This new one, I am not sure."

Wanda cocked her head. "I believe you're right. The 'd' is a bit different. Slanted, almost cursive like. And the 'o's' are rounder. Great observation, Ev!"

She gave her next door neighbor a high five. Evelyn lowered her eyelashes in a rare act of humility.

"Isaac said the first two were by different people. His expression made me wonder at first, but if he's telling the truth—and I believe he is—that means two people are involved in the graffiti markings. The question is, did the same person spray the first and the fourth or are we looking for three people?"

"We need the police copy of the first to determine that."

"Right. Todd has one in his phone. Perhaps we could invite him for pie, and I could . . ."

"Wanda!"

Her turn to feel contrite. "You're right, that would be prying. Well, let's invite him anyway. Maybe he will show us the first one."

Evelyn folded her arms over her chest and sat back. "Much better."

Wanda winked and called Todd.

Buttermilk Pie

This recipe is my own version of a recipe I adapted from the 1888 "Household Manual and Practical Cookbook" by the Ladies of St. Paul's Episcopal Church, Waco, TX.

Ingredients:

- 2 c. buttermilk - You can substitute ¼ c vinegar and 1 ¾ c regular milk but it leaves a slight aftertaste.
- 1 ½ c. sugar
- ¼ tsp. salt
- ½ c unsalted butter – Don't use margarine, it won't have the same consistency or flavor.
- 3 eggs
- 3 Tbsp of flour

- ½ tsp. Mexican vanilla - It is so much richer than vanilla extract, so if you can find it, use it!
- ¼ tsp. of almond extract
- I add 3 shakes ground cinnamon for a zest of flavor.
- One unbaked pie crust

Directions:

1. Preheat oven to 350 degrees.
2. In a large bowl, blend the flour, sugar, and salt together. I use a fork instead of a spoon. Cream in the butter, a chunk at a time until it sort of looks like lumpy oatmeal. Then mix in eggs one at a time until it is smooth – no more lumps!
3. Finally, add in the vanilla, almond extract, and if you wish, the cinnamon.
4. Prick the bottom of of the raw crust with a fork so it cooks evenly, but be careful not to tear it or punch all the way through.
5. Here's a trick my grandmother taught me: To keep the bottom crust from getting soggy, set the crust by placing it in a preheated oven for five minutes, then carefully remove it and pour the filling inside.
6. Return to the oven and bake for 40-45 minutes. You know it is done when you can insert a toothpick in the center, and it comes out clean.

Chapter Seventeen

"Sure, I can take a break. I love your buttermilk pie. Be there in five."

Wanda's smile stretched into her cheeks. She couldn't help it. She loved that boy. "He's on his way."

He arrived with a tippity-tap-tap-tap on her backdoor, their mutual signal, and then entered. He stopped as his gaze hit the pictures laid out on the table.

"Aha. I knew there was an ulterior motive to your invite." He removed his Stetson and sat down. "To answer your question before you ask. Yes, the fourth one resembles the handwriting of the first one. See?"

He held out his phone. "I'll email it to you. Doubt that is breaking the rules at this point."

Evelyn winked at her and mouthed, "See, you didn't have to ask."

Wanda waggled her head as Todd's thumbs danced over his phone pad.

A few minutes later, a photo of all four lay across her table along with a few piecrust crumbs.

"Well?" He glanced at each of them. "Thoughts?"

Wanda stared at the images for a moment and then glanced at her nephew. "Do you believe they are related to what happened to Shari?"

He rocked back in his chair, something Wanda hated. Why did men do that anyway? Balance on the back two legs. So precarious. Perhaps that was why.

"Jury's still out on that one. There have not been any more assaults. It very well may be a gang moving in, and Shari disturbed one of them."

"And the van driver?" Evelyn downed the last bite of her pie and stood to put the plate in the sink.

"Speculation. He got freaked when he saw Shari being assaulted, dropped the crates, and skedaddled?"

Wanda shook her head. "I don't buy it. He knew the transport had been in an accident. Heck, he may be the original driver for all we know."

"That is true. He is still missing in action." Todd returned his chair legs to the floor and dug into his pie. With a half-full mouth, he continued. "We know who he is. The family has not seen nor heard from him."

Wanda rested her chin in her hand. "Name now one man." Then she sat up straight. "The driver. They are daring us to figure out who he is."

"For what reason?" Todd peered at her over his coffee

mug.

"Shari isn't telling, that's for sure."

"You think she knows who he is, don't you, Aunt Wanda."

"Betty Sue gave me the impression that you both did."

He tilted his hand back and forth to indicate he couldn't be certain. "What do you two make of the other messages? I don't get the second one other than it was on the liquor store wall."

Evelyn narrowed her eyes as if searing it into her brain would reveal a hidden message. Wanda remained silent and let her friend's gears turn. After all, she was the mystery novel buff. When they watched whodunits on TV, Evelyn usually had it figured out halfway through the show.

"Could Red Rum be a code name? I mean isn't rum usually clear or brown?"

Todd did a search on his phone. "Ha. Red rum is murder spelled backwards. First appeared on the mirror in the book and the movie, *The Shining*."

Evelyn ran her hands up and down her arms. "Oooh. I saw that one decades ago. Scary movie. Jack Nicholson, right?"

Todd grunted. "It is also the name of a famous British racehorse. Doubt that has anything to do with this, though."

Wanda gazed at the photo. "So, 'redrum sir, is murder' is simply telling us that it is a palindrome."

"So is murdrum. That's the murder of a person

unknown to the killer, right, Todd?"

Evelyn appeared rejuvenated, but whether by the caffeine and sugar or the case before them Wanda couldn't tell.

"Yep." He turned off his phone. "Except there hasn't been a murder this time."

"Unless . . ." Wanda leaned forward and tapped the picture with her fingernail. "The driver has been killed and the county sheriff's department simply hasn't discovered his body."

"Then the van driver at the grocer's took his place, delivering only four crates." Todd wiggled his eyebrows.

"One of which had a powdery substance in it. Has forensics gotten back with you?"

Todd shook his head. "They probably will tomorrow. Even if it is drugs, there is no proving it was hidden among the veggies."

"Would they still be in the dumpster?" Wanda's pulse increased. To find drugs on kale along with spray cans would cinch this case. Maybe Betty Sue would never eat the stuff again.

"Not a chance. Trash truck came yesterday. Recycle comes tomorrow."

Wanda's hopes slumped to her toenails.

Evelyn whispered under her breath. "There goes our morning adventure."

"What?" Todd turned to her.

She winced when Wanda kicked her under the table. "Nothing."

Todd quirked his eyebrows but kept quiet except asking if he could have the last piece of pie.

Well, he's young and has the metabolism of a cheetah, Wanda thought to herself. "Sure. Better on your hips than mine."

The three sat in silence while he finished his treat.

A beep sounded. Todd glanced at his phone and his face paled. "Gotta get, ladies" He rose, kissed Wanda on the cheek, thanked her for the pie, and grabbed his hat.

A few seconds later they heard his cruiser zip down the street.

"What was that all about?" Evelyn grabbed his plate, fork, and mug to put in the sink.

Wanda gathered the rest of the dishes. "They just found a body in a shallow grave. Guess the coyotes dug it up."

"Howja know?"

A smirk oozed across Wanda's lips. She couldn't help it. "Over the past year I have learned to read his phone messages upside down."

"You do beat all." Evelyn's cackle woke Sophie from her slumber.

Chapter Eighteen

Animated discussion marked the neighborhood watch captain's special meeting in the senior adult's classroom at Holy Hill Church. Not only the graffiti epidemic, as Henry Hampton described it, but also the fact that a citizen had been attacked in an alley stirred emotions.

"We have all used the alley to cut through town, and though they can be a bit smelly in the summer . . ."

Chuckles floated in the room.

Henry continued, ". . . they have always been safe. Many of us use that short cut to take our tills to the bank."

Wanda raised her voice over the murmurs. "Yes, about that. I am not sure it is wise to carry bank bags anymore. That's why they have a well-lit night drop with a camera. Perhaps it is better to drive up after store hours and drop it off."

Some nodded but a few pouted.

Frank Patterson hacked and then cleared his throat.

"Don't y'all have drop safes? My grandson works at that large home improvement store out on the highway and they have one. It would be a worthwhile investment to get one."

Someone groaned. Wanda couldn't tell who. She turned to the man who still had the floor.

"Henry, you are the captain of the downtown watch corridor. I suggest you organize a time when your watch people can accompany the merchants like yourself to the bank. I know Mr. Garza walks to the bank as well. Perhaps all meet up and go as a group. The adage of safety in numbers, you know."

"Perhaps. I'll talk to my watch people. But I have been taking the evening and morning till at noonish to the bank for thirty some odd years. Seems a shame to have to change now because our town is growing, and the big city dwellers are moving in." Henry sat down.

Wanda smiled and counted to three before answering. "Like it or not, we no longer live in the 1980s. That is why we formed this watch, right?"

Several agreed. A few crossed their arms over their chests, not a good sign.

Jerry Suntych, a retired police officer from Houston, stood. "As one of those big city dwellers, I can tell you I moved here to get away from the crime. But it seems to have followed. Wanda is right. We need to adjust."

Fred Ballinger, the retired principal who always smiled extra sweetly at Betty Sue, spoke up. "Common values are a thing of the past. We can't teach them to the students anymore. Heck, we get grief from some of these parents for saying the Pledge of Allegiance now."

"And no one teaches the youth about sin and the Bible. We need to get more of them into church." Henry held up a forefinger to make his point.

Claps sounded.

And on it went for another fifteen minutes—how the world was going to *you-know-where* in a handbasket.

Wanda's temples began to ache. She refrained from massaging them. Then her ears perked up.

Out of the corner of her eye Wanda saw a message pop up on her phone. Todd.

Body ID'd as produce driver.

Chapter Nineteen

Wanda banged her knuckles on the table to get everyone's attention. Ow. She really needed to purchase a gavel.

"People. I just got word from the police department. There has been a murder outside of town."

The room became stone still.

Jerry stood. "Who?"

"The organic produce driver who was supposed to deliver the crates of veggies to the Grocery Mart. Shari had been pacing on her grand opening day because the 7:00 a.m. delivery never arrived. About nine, she heard a diesel engine and went out back to the alley. The next thing we knew, she had been attacked. Later that day, the county police found the delivery van upturned on a county road with the driver missing." She let out a long sigh. "Now it appears he isn't missing anymore. Let's bow our heads and pray for his family."

All the heads in the room tilted downward, most of the men removed their caps first.

After a minute Wanda said the amen and then continued, now that she had everyone's attention. "We don't know the timeline, but I think someone hijacked the driver and then impersonated him in another van. The rest of Shari's order is accounted for at the scene. Yet next to her slumped body lay four crates of veggies, one of which later had an unknown powdery substance in the corner."

Fred gasped. "You mean drugs?" As past principal of the high school, that was probably his number one fear.

"We don't know. It has been sent to the county lab for . . ."

"Hey, wasn't she fresh from drug rehab?" Henry scanned the room for confirmation.

"Yeah, Priscilla persuaded Collin to take her on. Looks like a mistake to me." Frank wheezed in disgust. Frank had several different coughs and wheezes, most of which Wanda had learned to interpret over many years of being his backyard neighbor.

Murmurs of agreement rippled through the attendees.

Here we go. She pumped her hands. "People. People."

Evelyn, who had been silent up to this point whistled through her teeth. "Let Wanda speak."

"Thanks, Ev. In this country we are supposed to be innocent until proven guilty, right? You know my history with my own daughter. I am not naïve when it comes to addicts, but let's try to not jump to conclusions."

Betty Sue raised her hand. "One of the crates contained squash, and squash leaves can develop a powdery mildew. It could very well be organic."

"I didn't know that." Wanda turned to her. "Maybe I need to text Todd."

"Sorry. I recalled it later today when making that squash dish. I'll bring it by for lunch."

Wanda returned her focus to the meeting. "Okay. All in favor of beefing up patrols in downtown say aye."

Positive responses filled the room.

"Sectors one, two, and three, poll your volunteers and see if any of them can take a day shift in sector four. Then contact Henry so he can make up a chart of times. I will keep you posted on any further developments. In the meantime, can everyone meet back here after services tomorrow for a quick briefing? I should know more by then."

Most of them nodded that they could.

"Good. Eight o-clock, but we'll keep it brief, agreed?" She didn't need any lengthy tangents of discussion. From the expressions on their faces, she figured they got her drift. "Now, I want to end this meeting by saying a prayer that I found on the internet for first responders. They all need it these days."

Once again, heads bowed. At the end of the prayer the captains shuffled out. Evelyn and Betty Sue stayed. Betty

Sue's face showed worry lines.

"I better go see Priscilla and let her know what people said. Shari is in for a rough time."

"It may now get rougher. Especially if the lab results are not squash mildew." Wanda closed her notebook and pushed in her chair.

"You think she is involved in drug smuggling, don't you?" Betty Sue's tone turned edgy.

Wanda lifted one shoulder. "You agreed she either lied or withheld information about her attacker. Why else would she do that?"

Betty Sue halted. "Fear. Intimidation. She had been assaulted, you know."

Evelyn stepped between them. "Wanda, let's not speculate yet. Like you said, innocent until proven guilty."

"Okay. Let's go." Wanda lifted her purse to her shoulder. She figured she better patch the growing tensions in the room by offering an olive branch to her old friend. "Betty Sue, I would love some of your squash dish for lunch tomorrow."

Her friend's face lit. "Of course. I will bring it by, and we can share. Evelyn you are welcome to join us. Say noonish?"

"Sure, okay."

From her forced grin, Wanda knew Evelyn felt trapped. A meat and potatoes gal, her diet rarely deviated. How *did* she stay so skinny? Maybe someday soon scientists would invent a metabolism transplant. She could only pray.

The three walked to their cars in silence. After Betty Sue drove away, Evelyn put her hand on Wanda's arm. "You okay?"

"Sure, why?"

"All this talk of drugs and rehab. I know it dredges up stuff. How is Wesley?"

"All right, I guess. I haven't heard from her, so that may be a sign all is well. It seems she only calls when she's in crisis."

Evelyn side hugged her, an unusual gesture.

Wanda stiffened. "What gives? I mean I know you're my friend and we share things, but why the huggy-feely?"

Evelyn glanced away at the streetlight. "I don't know. The past year or so it seems this town has seen so much turmoil. We thought the influx of young folk would boost it, but so far it has done the opposite." She jerked back. "Not to say people Todd's age are all bad. Don't get me wrong. It is just their values are not like ours. Often, I mean . . ."

Wanda leaned her backside against her car. "Todd is worried because crime has increased since he came."

"What? You mean his job is on the line? That's absurd."

"No, I don't think so. Not after the accommodation the mayor gave him over the Ferguson Mansion case. But he feels that eyes are on him."

Evelyn made a raspberry with her lips. "Of course, they

are. He's the one solving these crimes, thanks to us." She winked and elbowed Wanda in the ribs.

Wanda laughed. "You're right. So, let's get to the business of helping to solve this one."

"Atta girl. Let's concentrate on the palindromes. I still think they contain the key."

"Agreed. Let's head back to my place."

They got in Wanda's car. As she drove around the back of the church to head up 7th Street, her headlights hit the rear of the education wing. A new palindrome had been scrawled in blue on the wall.

Wanda slammed on her brakes. Dust mites danced in her car beams, which she aimed directly at the building.

"Dennis sinned." The two read out loud in unison.

"Better get Pastor Bob. And Todd." Wanda grabbed her phone from her purse.

Pastor Bob's rectory lay across the street at Cedar and 6th Street. He dashed over in his navy sweats. Todd arrived in his cruiser within minutes and jogged over to where they stood.

"See?" Wanda pointed to the sprayed scrawl. Her finger shook slightly with anger.

"Who is Dennis?"

Pastor Bob shook his head. "No one in my flock."

Wanda stepped up. "Not the driver of the produce van by any chance?"

Todd let out a nervous snicker. "If only it would be that

simple."

She waited but he didn't reveal the victim's identity. Most likely he'd remain tightlipped until the next of kin had been notified. Guess she'd have to wait for the article in *The Oakmont County Gazette*, if the police released the name by printing time on Thursday night.

"Well, Aunt Wanda. Same handwriting?"

She took a picture and then scrolled to the others. "I'm hardly an expert, but I'd say it is with number one and four. Agreed?'

The two men stared into her phone, their facial features eerily exaggerated by its glow.

Pastor Bob shrugged. "I guess so. They are more flowing in style. When can I get to work removing this?"

"Not for a day or so, okay? I think we were premature with Collin." Todd walked over to his cruiser to get his camera.

"Why blue?" Wanda placed her fist under her chin as she rested her elbow on her other arm.

"Excuse me?"

"Pastor Bob. Does blue have a liturgical significance?"

"It is the color of purity and honesty. True blue and all that. The Virgin Mary is often pictured in a blue robe."

Wanda puzzled over that. Perhaps *Dennis*, which is sinned backwards, was a red herring. *No make that a blue herring*. It may not be a real person at all. The real emphasis would be on the word sinned.

Her brain flashed back to the captains' conversation in the education room that evening. The windows had been opened to let the cool breeze in. Who had been eavesdropping?

The paint appeared fresh. She could smell the aerosol as well as detect a few runs glistening on the building. The church had spotlights, but this corner of the building remained in semi-darkness. Up until now, it had never been an issue.

She swiveled on her heel to locate the nearest light, and as she did something caught her eye in the beam of her headlights. She walked over to the edge of the fence where tufts of grass peeked through.

"Todd. Found something."

In the dirt was a partial footprint and another, as if someone had been standing across the alleyway, observing the meeting. Goosebumps raced up her spine.

Todd took a photo of them, and as his flash lit the scene, she noticed a tread in the soles. "Runners?"

He crouched down. "Appears so. I think I can almost detect part of the brand name that they often stamp on the ball of the sole. By the tread, my guess is they are running shoes."

"Men's?"

He stood and glanced at the underside of his size 11 boots. The footprint appeared smaller. "Or a large woman's foot. This must be a nine and a half, at least. Better rope it off and call it in."

Todd patted his aunt's shoulder. "Good catch." Then he left to get crime scene tape out of the trunk.

"I don't like this at all."

Wanda jolted at the sound of a deep male voice, not realizing who had walked over to her. "E . . . excuse me, Pastor?"

Pastor Bob's face blanched. "Sorry. Didn't mean to scare you."

"It's all right. We're all on edge." She huffed a long breath to ease the tightness in her chest.

"I said I don't care for this at all. Oh, the graffiti in itself is harmless. In fact, I could add to it. 'But Jesus saves.' Or something like that."

"Except this may be a crime scene."

"That's what I don't like, Wanda, my dear." He laid a pastoral hand on her shoulder. "I'm going in the sanctuary to pray in case anyone needs me."

Wanda gulped as she whispered okay and watched the usually strong shepherd of her flock walk away with his hands dug deep into his sweatpants pockets. No one likes to see a church defaced, but his reaction ran deeper. Had he figured out their meeting had an unwelcomed eavesdropper, too? Or did he know something else?

Evelyn wandered over.

Wanda had almost forgotten she had been in the car with her. "You okay?"

"Yeah." She motioned to the grassy area with her chin. "What is it?"

"We, I mean I, found footprints. Looks like jogging shoes."

"Where?"

"There." Wanda indicated a spot only a few feet beyond them with her forefinger. She twisted around and pointed to the building. "Right opposite the open window in the classroom where we were meeting tonight."

"That's disconcerting."

"Yeah. Isn't it?" She watched Todd return and wind the tape around the area to cordon it off.

A cold stone settled in her midriff. This place had been her home of worship since her family moved here when she was in elementary school. The atrocity of vandalizing something so near and dear to her heart tugged at her gut.

Much less being spied upon while in a meeting about securing the town's safety. Talk about a slap in the face. Whoever this person or persons turned out to be, by watching her they had just torpedoed her standing in the community as chairperson of the neighborhood watch committee. The irony of it stirred her emotions until they bubbled up to her throat.

"How dare they? This is no longer amusing." She stomped her foot and strutted to her car.

Evelyn scurried to keep pace. "What are you going to do?"

Wanda clicked the fob. "Solve the meaning of this palindrome series. That's what. You coming?"

"Sure." Evelyn climbed into the passenger seat and clicked her belt. "I'll call Betty Sue and fill her in."

"Let's do this, then." Wanda clenched her teeth as she started the ignition. Even if she stayed up all night, she'd figure this thing out. It had now become personal.

Chapter Twenty

Betty Sue met them in the driveway. “I brought spiced carrot cake. Don’t worry, it’s healthy.”

Wanda almost hugged her. She opened the backdoor and flicked on the kitchen light. Sophie blinked and stretched. Her long doggie yawn reached almost down her dachshund body to her tail.

“Sorry to wake you. Wanna go out?” Wanda stepped aside as the dog waddled by and plopped one by one down the stoop steps.

She smirked. “I love that old hound. Ladies, come in.”

They entered and gathered around the dinette where the other pictures still lay.

Wanda put on a kettle of water to boil, then took out her phone. “I’ll print this latest one off and be back in a sec.”

When she returned, Betty Sue already had placed slices of carrot cake on plates. The kettle whistled.

Wanda got down the tin of tea bag selections, some herbal, some flavored. “Pick your poison, ladies.” She took a spiced decaffeinated one, then changed her mind and chose an English breakfast tea. She'd need the boost to her brain cells.

Sophie slithered through the doggie door flap and resettled in her bed by the fridge. Wanda shook her head. "She will use it to come back in but wants me to open the door for her to go out."

Evelyn chuckled. "And you dutifully obey. Pets. They know who's the real master."

The women sat at the table as Wanda put a half forkful of carrot cake in her mouth. "Yum." She mumbled with her hand to her mouth. "Betty Sue, is this healthy?"

Evelyn raised her plate and sniffed it.

"It is. I make it with unsweetened applesauce and Stevia." She leaned toward Evelyn. "A natural sweetener, like sugar but better for you."

"Good because that saccharin stuff is bitter." She set her plate down and bravely forked a piece. Then she bobbed her a head in approval when it hit her tongue.

Betty Sue grinned as her eyes twinkled. To win over Evelyn's culinary preferences meant a lot.

Already Wanda felt better. Having her friends around her table enjoying dessert and tea made things a bit nicer. But they had a task to accomplish.

"Let's lay these out side by side as if in a sentence." She arranged the notecards after writing the last message on a blank one. "We can compare handwriting styles later. I think the message at this point is more important. Agreed?"

Her friends did.

"I did, did I? Red rum, sir, is murder. Name now one man. Borrow or rob. Dennis sinned."

Betty Sue glanced up. "Who is Dennis?"

Evelyn sighed. "We haven't a clue."

"It's only eight-fifteen. Not too late to call." Betty Sue took her phone from her sweater pocket and punched in a number. "Priscilla. Hi. Listen. Ask Shari if she knows anyone named Dennis."

Wanda tapped her temple. Smart move. "If she does, ask if he is a jogger or a runner."

A few minutes later Priscilla responded. Wanda could hear her voice but not her words.

"Oh, okay thanks." Betty Sue smiled and nodded with the phone to her ear. "Nothing, just a new graffiti message. Talk later. Thanks."

"Well?" Wanda stared at her friend.

Betty Sue hung up, her eyes suddenly sorrowful. "Nope."

Evelyn scoffed. "That'd be too easy." She shuffled another piece of cake in her mouth.

Wanda thought. After a moment she sat back. "Any students you know named Dennis?"

"You think it is a high school gang?" Betty Sue took a sip of her chamomile tea.

"Well, maybe. I dunno. But drug dealers do recruit kids

with the lure of fast money." Wanda knew she grabbed at straws. Unless it was a dangling thread she grasped instead. That could then unravel the mystery. "Any you had in fifth or sixth grade before you retired would be high schoolers now, right?"

"True." Betty Sue rose to pace the kitchen floor.

Evelyn ate her cake.

Wanda bit her lip.

"I do recall one kid. Dennis . . . what was his last name?" She thumped her temple with her finger. "Oh, yes. Alberts. He graduated in 2016. Went to Rice University on a full scholarship if I recall correctly."

"Athletic?"

"No, Wanda. Geeky. All the way. President of the chess club, straight-As in math and sciences. Probably works for NASA now." She slumped back into her chair.

"Oh, well."

Evelyn piped up. "I know one."

"Who?" Betty Sue and Wanda chimed in at the same time . . . again.

"The Menace of course."

Wanda grimaced. "Ha, ha."

Evelyn shrugged and took her empty plate to the counter.

Betty Sue's eyes widened when she noticed Evelyn cutting herself another piece of cake.

Wanda stifled a giggle and finished her piece of dessert.

Then she dropped her fork back on the plate as her brain began to swirl.

"Wait. Why not?"

"Huh?" Evelyn sat back down with a full plate.

Betty Sue gave them both a blank stare.

Wanda snapped her fingers. "Evelyn, you're brilliant."

"I am?"

"Yes. A menace is a nuisance. A no-gooder. A person who can cause harm or injury. A sinner with a motive."

She texted Todd.

Got carrot cake and clues. Head this way. Quick before Ev eats it all.

He texted back.

Wow. Must be good. Ok. See you in ten. Need a break from speed trap anyway.

Wanda had almost forgotten he, as a small-town policeman, had other duties besides solving crimes. She chuckled and ended with a thumb's up emoji. "Todd is on his way over here. Let's save him a piece of cake."

"What have you come up with?" Betty Sue waggled her finger at Wanda. "I can tell by the look on your face you have figured something out."

"I recall a conversation I overheard between Collin and Miguel Garza, the son of the liquor store manager. Miguel complained of some girl who had only recently been hired and how she disrupted everything."

"And you thought he meant Shari." Evelyn pointed a

fork full of cake in her direction.

"Right, I did. Mr. Collins told him to keep it to himself and he'd handle it in his own way. His voice sounded very stern. It almost made me shudder."

"He always seems so jolly and friendly." Betty Sue pouted. "You're sure it was him?"

"Absolutely, because I saw him and Miguel come out of the office a few seconds later." Wanda glanced at each of her friends. "What if it wasn't Shari? Have you two noticed a new female employee?"

"Who happened to be named Denise? That would be way too simple." Evelyn sneered.

"Okay. Maybe not, but still. Could she be the menace who is leaving messages? Some of these do kinda look like a girl's handwriting."

Betty Sue shook her short curls until they bounced. "No, no. That doesn't make any sense. I know every worker and they have all been there at least six months or so. Eli, Angie, Buckley, and Sue. Walter the butcher. Oh, and Gloria in the bakery."

"She's right." Evelyn raised an eyebrow. "Besides, the police handwriting expert said a man wrote them, correct?"

Wanda gathered the photos on the table. "The second and third ones, yes. They seem to match but the first and last don't. See the letters are more roundish and the flow more fluid almost as if sprayed in one stroke. Like cursive writing."

Evelyn's eyes popped open. "Wait. You think the first and the last came from a female and a guy responded by writing two and three?"

"Possibly." She got the feeling they were teetering on the edge of figuring this all out. "Or they were made to appear that way to frame someone. I recall that Isaac and Miguel were assigned to paint the signs, so they would have known where the paints were stored. What if Miguel painted the other messages?"

"To what end?" A male voice made her jump.

Todd stood on her stoop, his hand on the knob of the open backdoor.

Wanda's hand flew to her mouth. "My word. You must stop doing that. Ever since you oiled those hinges that door is as silent as a ghost."

He laughed and headed for the counter. "Ah, a few pieces left. Who made it?"

Evelyn volunteered the answer. "Betty Sue. But it turned out really good."

Wanda pursed her lips to keep from laughing when she noticed the expression on Betty Sue's face.

Then Evelyn blushed. "That's not what I meant. Only that she made it healthy without all the sugar and stuff we are not supposed to have anymore."

"Ah." Todd grabbed a fork and shoveled some in his mouth, then his eyes widened. "Mmmm. This is good. I wouldn't know the difference." He leaned his backside against the edge of the sink. "So why am I here?"

"The last one. 'Dennis sinned.' It has me thinking."

He gazed at the ceiling. "I knew it." Then his focus returned to her face. "Okay. I admit, Aunt Wanda that often your thinking leads to something that makes a lot of sense so lay it on me."

She felt her cheeks warm at his compliment and rubbed one of them. "Well . . ." She scooted up in her chair. "We have laid out all of the palindromes thinking if we string them together, they might be more coherent than random. But the problem is that one, four and five appeared to be the same handwriting whereas two and three appear to be in a different one. Therefore, we surmised two people are graffitiing the town."

"Uh, huh." He shoved another piece of cake in his mouth.

"As I told the ladies here, I overheard Miguel complaining about a female employee to Collin. He said she'd been there only a few days and already cause disruption. I think he complained about Shari and from the tone in Collin's response I believe it was not the first time Miguel complained about her."

"Wait. When?" He halted the next bite halfway to his mouth.

"Later in the day."

He set his plate down. "You mean the day of Shari's assault?"

"Yes."

"And you didn't mention this because . . ." His forehead turned red.

"It didn't seem relevant at the time, or I would have said something to you."

The vein on his brow began to protrude, but he kept his cool. Total police mode, Wanda figured. Secretly she was glad her friends were present so he would remain professional and not chew her out in front of them. With that in mind, she ventured on with her thoughts.

"What if Shari found the paint and scrawled, 'I did, did I?' Maybe she didn't even realize it made a palindrome. But Miguel picked up on it and began spray painting other messages to frame her. Especially the 'name now one man.' It sounds as if he dared her. Then, when she felt better, she sprayed the last one, 'Dennis sinned.' Meaning Miguel was being a menace to her. She'd named the one man."

Evelyn chimed in. "What about the one that said, 'borrow or rob'?"

"That could mean a number of things, from the cans of spray paint to that funny white powder in the crates or even something we are not yet aware of." Wanda shrugged.

"No. It doesn't jive, Aunt Wanda. The next three were painted while Shari lay in bed."

"He's right, dear." Betty Sue placed a hand gently on Wanda's arm.

"Yeah. Why would the son of the liquor store manager

write a demeaning phrase on his dad's store?" Evelyn glanced at her then Todd.

Wanda's voice dropped in sync with her mood. "I thought perhaps he did it to frame Shari and may have done it the night before. How long does it take spray paint to dry?"

"Only a few hours on something as porous as brick. Besides, Mr. Garza told us he hadn't seen it earlier in the day." Todd pushed off from the counter. "But I'll talk with Miguel. If he has had a grudge against Shari, we need to know that. And I plan to ask Collin why he failed to mention it to us."

He nodded to each of the ladies then focused on his aunt. "Is there anything else you wish to tell me?"

"Not at the moment. Other than I love you." She gave him a motherly smile. Maybe reminding him of the fact would further diffuse the situation.

He blushed like a schoolboy and simply gave her a nod. Then, clearing his throat, he left.

Evelyn chuckled. "That was sly of you."

Wanda sighed and rose from her chair to take her plate to the sink. "I simply wanted to remind him I am doing this to help. My ways may be bumbling, but still . . ."

Betty Sue clucked. "We know that, and he does as well, dear friend. However, you must admit you love a mystery. You've always been a puzzle solver."

Wanda could do nothing but agree.

Healthier Carrot Cake

Ingredients:

Cake:

- 1 c. old-fashioned or quick-cooking oats
- 1 ¼ c. unsweetened applesauce – unflavored is best.
- 1 c. packed brown sugar – For even healthier, you may use Brown Swerve Stevia, but don't use Monk Fruit as it has an aftertaste when blended with the applesauce.
- 2 c. shredded carrots, about 4 medium-sized stalks
- ½ c. fat-free egg product or 2 eggs – Your choice, depending on whether you like low cholesterol options. Betty Sue does.
- 1/3 c. canola oil or avocado oil – No olive oil. The taste is too strong.
- 1 ½ c. Gold Medal™ whole wheat flour – You may want to try Carb-Quik. It is a lower carb substitute for Bisquick. If so, do not add the baking powder below.
- 2 tsp. baking powder
- 1 tsp. baking soda
- ½ tsp. salt
- 1 tsp. pumpkin pie spice
- ½ c. golden raisins
- ½ c. finely chopped nuts – Walnut or pecans work best.

Frosting:

- 4 oz. reduced-fat cream cheese, softened - Philadelphia Whipped Cream Cheese makes blending even easier.
- ¼ c. powdered sugar or use Swerve powdered Stevia
- 3 Tbsp milk - Fat free milk really doesn't work. 2% skim may, but reduce by 1 tsp.
- 1 tsp. vanilla

Directions:

1. Heat oven to 350°F. Spray 12-cup fluted tube cake pan with cooking spray.
2. In large bowl, mix oats, applesauce, brown sugar or Stevia substitute, carrots, egg product and oil with spoon until well mixed. Stir in remaining cake ingredients just until moistened. Pour into pan.
3. Bake 50 to 55 minutes or until toothpick inserted in center comes out clean. Cool in the pan on a baking rack for 10 minutes. Upturn the cake pan onto parchment paper draped over the rack and tap along the bottom with a wooden spoon, then shake very gently to loosen it from the pan. If some sticks to the bottom, don't panic. You can cover it with the icing.
4. Cool completely, about 1 hour.
5. In small-medium bowl, beat cream cheese and powdered sugar (or Swerve) with electric mixer on medium speed until smooth. Beat in milk and vanilla until well mixed. Place cake on serving plate. Spoon frosting over cake using a spatula.

Or you can leave the cake to cool entirely in the pan and then put a thicker layer of icing on just the top. If taking it to a potluck, as Betty Sue often does, it may be easier to transport this way and later cut into cubes and serve.

Chapter Twenty-One

Wanda may as well have been a chicken roasting on a spit as much as she turned in the night. Her bedclothes ended up almost mummifying her. At daybreak, she slowly unwound herself and sighed. They were no closer to solving this mystery than the day Shari received her wallop.

Maybe one of the watch captains would report something. She could only hope.

She flicked on the kitchen light and stared once more at the graffiti messages. As the machine pushed the hot water through the tiny white pod filled with coffee grounds, she moved the first, fourth, and fifth sayings together.

"I did, did I? Borrow or rob. Dennis sinned." She read them aloud three times then read the second and third. "Red rum sir is murder. Name now one man."

She recalled what Todd had researched. Murder is red rum backwards. In other words, pun intended, murder is murder no matter how you look at it.

Aha. Her brain began to tingle with excitement.

The driver of the delivery van. Why did he become a corpse? Because he didn't comply with the drug smuggling, or because he made money on the sly and endangered the operation? Motive aside, murder cannot be justified.

The drug lords were notorious for taking matters into their own hands. Did Shari recognize the driver from her past dealings? And so, he whacked her for recognizing him to be a drug dealer?

She imagined the possible scenario.

The driver shoved Shari. *You squealed, didn't you?*

Shari's voice floated through her mind. She pictured her angrily pointing to a shadowed figure. *I did, did I? Is that what you think? Then why? To borrow it from you or rob you blind? No, not me. And I can name the man who did. That menace sinned. Not me.*

Wanda knew what one clue might tie it all together. She needed to find the name of the driver and what role he had played in all of this. Assuming it was a guy. Had Todd said that? She couldn't recall.

She grabbed her purse and jacket then yanked the door open. A desperate whine halted her.

"Oh, Sophie. I'm sorry, girl." She set her stuff on the counter, poured the kibbles in the dog's bowl, and changed out her water. The clock read 8:02 as sunbeams floated through the kitchen window, highlighted by the shadow of bird wings flapping on the feeder as it swung from the oak tree.

The world had awakened. Time was a wastin'.

She snatched the note cards and headed out into the cool morning sunlight on a mission to wake her nephew, pump him for information, and suffer the consequences later.

Chapter Twenty-Two

Though she knew where Todd hid the extra key, she possessed too much common sense to use it and enter his domain unannounced. Instead, she stood on his stoop and phoned him.

A groggy masculine voice answered. "Aunt Wanda? You okay?"

"Rise and shine. I'm on your stoop with two cups of coffee and breakfast burritos. We've got work to do."

"We? Wait." Through the phone she heard his grumble and then his bare footsteps plodding toward her. The door creeped open a crack as bloodshot eyes squinted from the sun's brightness. "Why did I pick an apartment that faced east?"

"Good question." Wanda nudged her way inside and set the take-out breakfast on his counter. Then she washed her hands vigorously and got down two plates, also scrubbing them . . . just in case. She nodded her head toward the food.

"Come sit. I'll give you three minutes to become cognitive."

The disheveled nephew slithered over and took his breakfast from her, then plopped on the sofa, amidst what she hoped was clean but yet-to-be-folded laundry. He took a sip of the hot caffeine and pointed at her with his burrito. "This better be good."

"Oh, it is." She knelt down, shoved the papers and pizza box from his coffee table, and slapped down the notecards in two groups as if she dealt the poker hand of a lifetime. "Read them."

Wanda rocked back on her heels and watched his mouth silently move. Then his eyes grew wider.

"Yes. It's a conversation. Between two people. My guess is a woman and a man." At least in her head the voices sounded male and female.

"And you have an idea who they might be?"

"I'm not sure. But something tells me the driver of the van is the key to unlocking this mystery's door. We know Shari is not telling us everything. You and Betty Sue both sensed it. I think she knew the original driver, saw it wasn't him, put two and two together, and got whacked." She finally took a breath, then wished she hadn't gotten so low to the floor. Getting up might prove awkward.

Todd bobbed his head. "The substitute driver would know she'd figure out he wasn't who she expected. He whacked her to silence her."

"But when he learned she had survived, somehow he got to her and threatened her to shut her up. Then he killed the driver to cover his tracks?"

Todd yawned. Loud and long. "This is starting to sound like a TV plot. Did you really need to wake me up at this ungodly hour?"

"Every hour is from God, Todd Martin. It is up to us to utilize it."

He rubbed his eyes. "And I had planned to use it rejuvenating my cells while I slept." Then he must have detected the disgruntlement in her eyes because he conceded. "Okay. Where do we go from here?"

"I think we need to have a nice, long chat with Shari. Away from her sisters' ears. Any word from the lab about the white powder?"

"Coke. High grade. Someone smuggled it amidst the veggies. We've called in the North Texas OCDETF." He popped his neck, and then bit into his burrito.

"Who?"

"Organized Crime Drug Enforcement Task Force." He spoke with his mouth half-full then swallowed. "It is a multi-agency effort in the war on drugs that works with the Feds. Someone organized the hijacking of the delivery van. Our guess from the coroner's report on the defensive wounds is the driver put up a fuss and refused to be involved. It cost him his life. One bullet in the forehead. End of story. Neat, clean and definitely professional." He bit off another piece of his breakfast wrap and chewed it for a moment. Then he pointed the rest of it at her nose. "And you are not to breathe a word of this to anyone. Not yet. Got it?"

Wanda nodded.

"But you're right. Shari may open up to us if we tell her the Feds are on the way to interrogate her. I doubt she wants to go back to the Lane Murray Unit in Gatesville. They won't be gentle with her this time, especially if she is into drug trafficking again."

"You think she is?"

He shoved the last piece of breakfast in his mouth and chased it with the coffee. Then he rose. "One way to find out. Back in a minute."

Todd headed for his bedroom and then stopped. "Aunt Wanda?"

"Yes?"

"Don't rush around cleaning things, okay."

He knew her too well. "I promise. I will only help you clean up the crime in this town."

Todd cocked an eyebrow then shook his head and disappeared. A moment later she heard the screech of the water taps in his shower.

Wanda gazed around the living space that reminded her of an upturned residence in the movies after the mob had hunted for the incriminating evidence the stool pigeon had hidden. Closing her eyes, she sat on her hands and sighed. She'd probably need his help getting off his carpet anyway. She tried to visualize what happened in that alley.

Was Shari a stool pigeon or a vulture? Did she pick that produce service for their extracurricular activities or discover it later when another driver showed up?

Then she sat upright. Wait! Speaking of . . . why had Todd still not told her the identity of the dead driver. What was up with that?

Chapter Twenty-Three

Wanda expected Todd to emerge in uniform, but he didn't. Wearing jeans and a long-sleeved knit shirt, he motioned at the door. "You coming?"

She raised her hand for him to help her up. He sighed, and grabbed on, giving her a yank as she scrambled to her feet.

"Let's go." He bounced down his steps.

Oh, to be young again. She shuffled after his long purposeful stride toward Unit Number 5. He stopped at the steps and pointed his finger at her face. "I do the talking, okay?"

"It's impolite to point, Todd. But okay. Then, why I'm there?"

"A witness, if needed. Though I will be recording this." He patted his front shirt pocket where his cell phone hid. Then she noticed his badge clipped to his jeans loop. "And you are a doting, friendly, female presence which may help

Shari open up a bit. Follow my lead."

She ignored the doting part and nodded in agreement.

He winked. Then he rapped his knuckles on the door.

Priscilla answered. "Yes? Todd?"

"We are here to speak with Shari."

The elder sister clenched her hands to the door. "Um, she isn't decent right now."

Todd stepped forward. "Then get her decent. The next knock will be the Drug Task Force. I am hoping to avoid that unpleasantry for her."

Priscilla's face turned red then stark white. "Right. Come in." She ran her hand through her hair, cast her gaze to the ground, and opened the front door.

The two entered. Wanda took a seat on the sofa.

Todd remained standing.

In a few minutes after several hushed and rushed words, Shari emerged in a bathrobe. Her eye appeared less colorful, now more shadowed in purple. The stitches still twisted through her skin.

"You, um, wanted to speak with me?"

Todd bobbed his head sharply and motioned with his hand for her to have a seat next to Wanda on the couch. He set his phone on the coffee table. "I have to record this."

She pursed her lips and gave him a quick nod.

He turned to Priscilla. "Can you kindly wait in the bedroom?"

She opened her mouth to protest, or so Wanda figured.

If in Priscilla's position, she would. But the stern expression in Todd's eyes must have changed the older sister's mind. Her body language shifted from defiant to compliant and she quietly shuffled away.

He waited until he heard the door click closed and then grabbed a chair from the dinette set and carried it over to sit across from the two women. Next, he tapped his phone to awaken the recording app. He reported the day and time and who was present. Only then did he make direct eye contact with the interviewee.

Wanda felt the girl's body stiffen against the sofa cushion next to her.

Todd's mouth softened into a small grin. "Shari, I'm not in uniform. This is an unofficial visit. But I want you to know if you refuse to cooperate the next one will be official and not by me or anyone here in Scrub Oak. It'll be the Drug Task Force."

The already sickly-looking face paled even more. "Why?"

"Those four crates of veggies? Coke residue turned up on one of them."

She became animated. "I don't know anything about that."

"You don't?"

She shook her head so violently it made her winch as she clutched her face on the side of the wounded temple.

Wanda bit her lip then whispered to Todd. "May I get

her some water?"

"Yea. Get us all some. Please."

Wanda rose, tiptoed into the kitchen, and found some glasses to fill with tap water. When she returned, Shari sat with her legs tucked under her, a throw pillow clutched to her chest, and her focus on the carpet.

Todd mouthed a thank you and took two of the glasses, slipping one across the coffee table in front of Shari.

A shaky hand reached for it. As the girl sipped, Todd placed the note cards on the table in the order that Wanda had arranged them at his place.

"What do you know about these? Take your time."

She glanced at him and then the cards. Her eyebrows scrunched together. "Are these supposed to mean something?"

"You tell me, Shari."

She opened her mouth then closed it again and shrugged.

Wanda decided the girl really had no clue or she had developed a great talent for lying, which she very well could have. Many who have traipsed on the other side of the law had developed that skill.

Todd tapped the first card. "Freshly written within inches of where you collapsed in that alley. That scar on your temple is from a spray paint can."

"And it knocked me out. So how would I know?" Her words hissed through clenched teeth.

In professional interrogation mode, Todd took another route to diffuse the emotion. "Do you know what these are? They all have a pattern that connects them. They read the same forward and backwards."

She squinted and mouthed the words, figuring out the sequence. Then she glanced up to his face. "Weird."

"We believe these are somehow connected to your assault. Shari, did you know the driver who originally had arranged to deliver your produce?"

"I'd met him a few times when deciding which service to go with, why?"

"And when you saw the guy in the van wasn't him, how did you react?"

She flashed him a dumb expression. "Well, duh. I asked who the heck he was."

"You were angry."

She answered in the affirmative, laced with a few less than lady-like adjectives. Then her cheeks flushed. "Sorry, Mrs. Warner. I forgot you were present."

"Thank you, and it's Wanda." She shifted her eyes to Todd as if to ask if this could be her entrance into the conversation, and he gave her a very slight nod.

"Shari, I don't want to upset you. Priscilla and Sally have told me about your past. You see, I have a daughter who has battled drug addiction as well."

Shari turned to Wanda, and her eyes held an emotion—sorrow, perhaps empathy. Her shoulders slacked a bit.

"Here's the thing, though. An investigation discovered a residue of cocaine in the corner of one of the crates. I think the one with beets. Not sure. Anyway, we believe the Feds will put it together and think you were trafficking."

"What?" Her lower lip quivered. It soon spread to her hands and then her whole body. A guttural groan blasted from her partially opened mouth and ended in a long wail, along with a stream of tears. "No, no, no, no."

Priscilla dashed out and crouched next to her, drawing her to her. Her eyes flashed at Todd. "How dare you?"

Todd didn't budge.

Wanda wiggled on the sofa cushion not knowing what to do. She finally reached across and grabbed a box of tissues off the coffee table.

Shari took several and began to dab her eyes. Her breathing turned to small hiccups and then slowly settled into regular breaths mixed with a few shudders.

Todd leaned in and replied in a calm, steady voice. "You need to tell us everything, Shari. This is your one shot before they pound on the door."

Her red-rimmed eyes lifted to meet his. "I'm clean. I swear."

"Prove it, Shari. If anyone is trying to pin something on you, let us know about it."

Her eyes grew wide and wild. "I honestly don't know." It came out in a whisper.

How many times had Wanda witnessed this scenario? Shari's face morphed into Wesley's. Her heart ached anew as she blinked several times to refocus on this room, this couch.

Todd sighed and sat back. Did he think the same thing? Were they both too close to a similar episode to be objective?

Priscilla raised up to her feet with daggers in her eyes aimed solely at him.

Wanda decided to intervene. She motioned for Priscilla to return to the bedroom with her, but the elder sister refused to budge so Wanda took a chance and spoke up.

"Todd is here as a friend, Priscilla. If we can get to the bottom of this and prove Shari is not involved, we can stop the Feds from dragging her out of here on suspicion of drug trafficking. I know you don't want them to ruin her shot at a new life. She deserves her chance, doesn't she?"

The woman blinked as if waking from a nightmare. She sighed and agreed. Wanda wrapped her arm around her and started down the short hall. But Priscilla stopped and swiveled back to half-face Todd.

"Don't upset her again. It could hamper her recovery."

"Noted." Todd set his jaw then shifted his focus to the sniffling Shari still dabbing her eyes.

Satisfied, Priscilla released herself from Wanda's grasp. "Think I'd rather take a walk, get some air."

She slipped out the front door, closing it softly behind

her.

Todd waited until her footsteps outside faded.

"Okay, Shari. She can't hear anything you say, and I promise it will stay with us. But I do need to keep the recorder on, for your benefit. Deal?"

She waggled her head a bit. Wanda guessed it was a compliant gesture, so she returned to sit next to Shari on the sofa.

Shari half-smiled and reached for Wanda's hand. Wanda took is in hers and patted it with her other hand.

Todd leaned in again, his fingers interlaced and resting on his knees. "Tell me what you said to the driver when you saw it wasn't the one you expected."

"Hey, who are *you*?"

"And his response?"

"He laughed."

"What did he wear?"

"I told you that when you interrogated me at the hospital. Jeans, a Ranger's baseball hat."

"Okay. What happened next."

"I caught a movement from the corner of my eye and an arm raised to meet me. Then whack. My head stung and the world went black."

"So, the driver didn't hit you. You're sure."

"I've told you all this, Todd. Why are you asking me again?" Her tone held agitation.

Wanda noticed she called him by his name not Officer

Martin. She wondered why. Because they were close in age? Did she recall him from high school? He would have been two years ahead of her.

She needed to ask Betty Sue or talk to Fred Balinger. Find out if Shari got in trouble in high school or afterwards. Something told her knowing that would be important.

"The other guy came out of nowhere. In a flash of light gray. It's all I recall. Honest."

Todd glimpsed at Wanda. Gray. Like the threads found in the crate and the description of the fleece jacket the graffiti artist wore. But gray was the in color in design and clothes so hardly a distinguishing clue. "You are certain it was gray? Not khaki green or light tan?"

"I think so."

"Do you recall how many crates he'd unloaded when you confronted the driver?"

"Maybe three or four? He held one in his hand when I asked who he was. The van had the side doors open."

"Color?"

"White." She stopped and thought. "Yes, white. And blank."

"Blank?" Todd narrowed his eyes.

"Yes. No writing. No name or logo. Like a rental or something."

His next sentence came out metered and slow. "Shari. The real van did a nosedive into a ditch about five miles outside of town."

"Oh, my gosh. Is Eduardo okay?"

Wanda flashed her eyes at Todd. His jawline moved slightly. So, Shari had known him well enough to know his name, and Todd had just wriggled that information out of her.

"No ma'am. He's dead."

Shari hugged herself as the tears fell afresh. "He was such a nice guy. Why him, God? Why him?"

Wanda locked eyes with Todd. He clicked off the app, pocketed his phone, and motioned for them to leave.

"Thanks, Shari. I will see what I can do to stave off the Feds."

She didn't respond, just turned her head to the wall and scrunched her knees to her chest.

The two rose and left the girl sniffling and crouched on the sofa. Outside in the balcony Wanda turned to her nephew. "Well, what's your impression?"

Todd stared out over the complex. "Not sure. She knew his name, though. And from her reaction, she knew him rather well. We are looking into his background." He slipped one boot onto the foot rail and leaned on the top one with his arms outstretched and hands clasped. "Did you know he went to school here?"

"He did? When?"

"Graduated a few years after me. Do me a favor. See what Betty Sue and Fred recall about him. Eduardo Espinoza."

"Will do. Todd?"

"Yeah?"

"For a moment it was déjà vu in there. You know?"

"Yep." He pushed off. "And Wesley never ever told us the truth either, did she?"

With that he plodded down the stairs back to his apartment.

Chapter Twenty-Four

Wanda called Evelyn and gave her a reprieve from Betty Sue's healthy lunch. "Todd wants me to pump info out of both Fred and Betty Sue. I figure over a meal would be the most congenial."

"Ah, to see if they can tell us about any kids who might have done the graffiti?"

"That and who Shari Wright hung out with in school."

"Have fun." Relief wrapped her response.

Hearing that Fred had been invited for lunch as well, Betty Sue brought over her spaghetti squash in one of her best serving dishes, garnished with parsley and sprigs of rosemary. But it wasn't what Wanda expected. It didn't look like spaghetti at all.

"Where are the meatballs?"

"These are squash boats. Kinda like a loaded baked potato. But you can use the rest of the spaghetti-like strands I gutted in other meals later. I brought you a bag of it. It lasts a good week or more in the fridge. Don't freeze it, though."

"Thanks." Wanda held up the plastic storage bag and tried not to scrunch her nose. "Caesar salad is on the table. Store bought kit. Is that okay?"

"Fine with me."

A tap-tap-tap sounded on the front door.

"Is that Fred?" Betty Sue had a quizzical expression. "Why didn't he come around back?"

"I don't think he's been invited inside before unless it was for a meeting. Just being polite I guess." Wanda went to let Fred in.

He offered her a bag of fresh rolls from the bakery. "Whole grain. Hope that's all right."

"They smell wonderful." Good, now she wouldn't starve on salad alone if Betty Sue's dish turned out to taste awful. "Come into the kitchen. We'll eat informally."

She weaved around the dining room set and turned back to make sure he followed. "Betty Sue's plating her new recipe. It looks really good."

Hearing her name, she glanced up.

Wanda saw Fred's smile widen and her friend's cheeks blush in response. They'd make such a cute couple. Both widowed, though Betty Sue much longer than him, they were also similar in age and past careers.

Wanda motioned for Fred to sit and then washed her hands and placed the rolls on a serving plate. Then she retrieved her butter tray and took the seat across from him leaving Betty Sue no choice but to sit beside him.

"Fred, I invited you both here for a reason. I wanted to pump your brains on a past student or two. But first, let's pray and serve the food. Fred, will you do the honors?"

After blessing the meal, Fred placed his napkin in his lap and waited for Betty Sue to serve him, which she did with the stately grace typical of Betty Sue. He gingerly forked some of the squash and tasted it. Immediately his eyes lit with delight. "Mmmm. Very nice."

Okay. Safe to try then. Wanda mimicked his actions and had the same reaction. "Betty Sue. This is actually quite delicious."

Then she realized what words had spewed from her mouth. She covered it with her hand and felt the heat rise from her neck into her cheeks.

Betty Sue laughed, as did Fred. Wanda joined in.

After a few minutes of small talk, Wanda decided to broach the reason for their gathering. She caught Fred up on the events in case he had not heard it all. "The driver was Eduardo Espinoza. Do either of you remember him?"

"I do." Fred wiped his mouth. "Nice kid. Single mother who worked as a cleaning lady at the medical center. He flipped burgers for Bob at Better Burgers a while in high school. Made good grades as I recall. Graduated in 2017?" He glanced at the ceiling as if it held the answer, then retuned his focus to Wanda. "Yes, that's right."

Wanda whispered it to herself a few times to brand it

into her memory.

"Didn't have the money for a university education but I think he took courses at Hill College in Burleson." Fred stopped and shook his head. "What a shame. Betty Sue, will you attend his funeral with me? I imagine they went to St. Joseph's in Cleburne."

Slick, Fred. Wanda almost winked at him.

Betty Sue glanced at her hands. "Of course. I remember him in elementary school. Quiet child, somewhat melancholy but never got into trouble." She raised her gaze again. "He always looked after his younger sister and was very protective of her. What was her name? Consuela?"

"Yes, she was three grades below him. And he had another little sister as well. Angelina, yes?" Fred snapped his fingers. "In fact, she might be attending the high school now. Maybe a junior?"

"Let's look her up and see." Betty Sue pulled out her phone and searched for the yearbook online.

Wanda leaned to read over her shoulder. "The yearbooks are digital now?"

"First time last year. They are trying it out. So far, the kids loved accessing it on their phone and pads. They can even sign them. Pretty cool."

"Technology." Wanda clucked her teeth.

Fred sat back. "Makes me kinda glad I retired when I did, though. I am way below the curve on that stuff."

"So, last year she'd have been a sophomore." Betty

scrolled. "Ah. Found her. Angelina Espinoza." She turned her phone for them to view her photo.

Wanda smiled. "She works at the Grocery Mart, doesn't she?"

Fred thought for a moment. "Yes, I do believe she might."

Betty Sue's eyes illuminated. "That's right. Angie. Of course."

The two locked eyes. Had they found the link to all of this? Could she be the girl who wrote half of the messages?

"Fred, when do the students learn about palindromes?"

"Not sure. Perhaps in fifth grade?"

Betty Sue knitted her forehead. "I don't think so. Onomatopoeia, synonyms, and homonyms, perhaps. But I think palindromes and word poems such as haikus would be taught later on."

"You are correct, as usual." He patted her hand then withdrew as if it had burned him. "Sorry."

She mumbled something to the effect of not minding it and glanced at her empty plate.

Wanda almost clapped with joy. Yep, the chemistry definitely floated between them. She had to find more reasons for them to be together, though Fred had already found one—attending the funeral. Though no one in their right mind would call it a date. How gruesome!

"Let me think. Yes, I believe sophomore English might cover that." Fred glanced away then back at the ladies.

"They study Shakespeare then, correct? Irony, symbolism, allegories and illusions, etc."

Wanda felt her lips spread into a smirk. She nodded to Betty Sue. Angie would have studied the word pattern last year, she had access to the spray cans, and possibly the storeroom. Had her actions somehow gotten her brother killed?

She decided she should attend the funeral as well. Maybe seeing how Angie reacted would shed some light upon her involvement. That wouldn't be wrong, would it? The detectives did it all the time on the cop shows she watched with Evelyn.

Chapter Twenty-Five

That afternoon Wanda called Tom Jacobs, the editor in chief of the *Oakmont County Gazette*. She wanted to find out if he knew when the funeral would be held and if the paper planned to run a story on the graffiti.

"Hi, Tom. Good to hear your voice on the other end again."

"Thank you. It is good to be back. Of course, I am letting the younger set really run things now. I stay here in case anyone drops in to chat while they hit the beat and scoop the stories."

Wanda held back a chuckle over his reporter lingo. "You heard about Eduardo Espinoza, right?"

"I did. We are running a small tribute to him in the upcoming addition on Friday. His funeral is Thursday, you know. St. Joe's in Cleburne. Three o'clock."

Those were the details she'd needed. "That is actually why I called. I figured if anyone would know it would be you."

He stuttered a thank you for her compliment. The man had always been a humble soul. "Did you know the family well?"

Always the reporter. If she had, she'd have known the funeral details. Tom Jacobs knew how to glean information. She sensed he really asked her why she wanted to know without coming right out with it. "No, just doing a little background work for Todd. I am trying to determine if the graffiti popping up around town is somehow related to Shari's assault and Eduardo's death."

He paused for a moment. Then he spoke again in a quieter, firmer voice. "Be careful, Wanda. Remember what happened to Evelyn."

"I will. Promise."

His tone became more serious. "You know there is a gang in Dallas who uses palindromes as secret messages, right?"

No, she didn't. "What's their name?"

He chuckled. "Oh, no. I am not telling you that. I know you, Wanda Warner. You'd grab Evelyn and Betty Sue and zip off to east Dallas. Get yourselves in all sorts of trouble. I don't want that on my conscience."

Ouch. That hurt. But then the truth often did.

"I did mention it to your nephew, though, when he phoned."

"You did, huh? And I suppose you can't tell me why

he called either?"

"Nope. Sorry. It wasn't to renew his subscription, though." He laughed.

Wanda ground her teeth. Oh, how he could wiggle under her skin. And he loved doing it. "Very funny, Tom."

His tone of voice warmed. "You know Misty and I both adore you. And we do thank you for all you did for our family a while back when crime darkened our door."

"My pleasure. If I do discover any connection between what happened to Shari and Eduardo and these palindromes, I will let you know. After I tell Todd, of course."

"Of course. Thanks, Wanda. Something tells me I will keep owing you and your neighborhood watch teams for long time. You keep the paper interesting. Glad you instigated the formation."

Now it was her turn to feel humbled. She thanked the editor and hung up.

Then she called Todd to fill him in on Angie. "What do you think?" she asked after giving him the low down.

"I think you are stretching it a bit. This is a small town. It is easy to make connections where none really exist."

He spoke truly. Kids needing a job either flipped burgers, sorted nuts, bolts, and screws for Henry, helped wipe tables at the Big B BBQ, or stocked the grocery shelves for Collin.

"So, I'm sniffing in the wrong gopher hole?"

"Can't say, Aunt Wanda. Just be careful. Eduardo's

death looked like a professional hit. The county guys are calling in the Feds now that drugs might be involved."

"That is just what Tom Jacobs told me as well. To be careful." She saw the break in the clouds and decided to fly through it. "Which reminds me, Todd. Exactly why did you phone him?"

"Gotta run. Talk later."

Click.

Hmm. Wanda stared at her phone's screen. A double denial and evasive maneuver. Now she definitely had to discover what was up.

Chapter Twenty-Six

Wanda and Evelyn walked down to the Grocery Mart. The warm day offered people a chance to shop outside on the curb for their fruits and veggies. Wanda told Evelyn all about her thoughts as they browsed the stands. "Well, what do you think?"

Evelyn shrugged as she searched through the leafy lettuce for the biggest one since they were priced by the head not the weight. "I'm still not sure, Wanda. It could have been about anything. Todd does have other cases, I'm sure. Maybe they're organizing a policeman's ball. You never know."

"Then why would Tom and Todd be so secretive?"

"Maybe to get your goat. I dunno." Evelyn faced her as she switched the shopping basket to her other arm. "Are you here to shop or snoop?"

"Both. I guess."

The aromas of oranges, grapefruit, and bananas did

entice Wanda's taste buds She took a paper sack from the rack, picked a few of each fruit, and placed them inside of it. "Are these organic?"

Evelyn moved on to the kiwis. "Don't think so. They'd say so if they were. Guess that grand scheme is on hold." Then she loudly cleared her throat and pointed with her head when she caught Wanda's attention. "Say, isn't that her?"

Wanda peered through the shoppers. A young woman with shoulder-length raven-colored hair slipped out of the store, took off her forest green grocer's apron, and dashed around the corner.

Wanda motioned to Evelyn. They set down their hand-held baskets and shoved them under the produce stand. Then the two women shuffled in the same direction the girl had headed and tiptoed to the edge of the building. They paused on the sidewalk once they had a view of the side street.

Halfway down the way, Angie talked with a young man in a gray fleece hoodie and jeans. Her body language suggested agitation or at the very least nervousness. The guy bent down with his hands on her shoulders and spoke to her as he gazed into her eyes as if trying to calm her. She nodded her head as she gazed to the ground. When he released his hands, she stood stone still, wiping her eyes.

Wanda heard a click and jolted. Evelyn had taken their picture with her phone.

The young man raised his gaze. Evelyn immediately

dug in her purse, replacing her phone. Wanda hovered over her as if helping her find something lost. She said in an extra loud voice, "I know you had the coupons when you left the house."

Evelyn, being quick witted, caught on. "Oh, dear. I am getting so forgetful these days. Did I put them in your purse instead?"

"Maybe." Wanda pretended to look through hers. Out of the corner of her eye she saw the young man back up and stroll away. Angie watched him cross the street and duck into an alley, then began walking back their way.

"Excuse me." Evelyn stopped her. "I can't find my coupons. Do you have extra copies from last week's paper?"

Angie jerked as if being startled and then cleared her throat. "Um yes, I think we have a few. I'll go get you one."

She dashed by them with her head ducked. But not before both ladies detected her red-rimmed eyes. The girl had been crying.

"Well, something upset her." Evelyn harumphed.

Well, she had just lost her brother, however Wanda wondered if it could be something else.

Then Evelyn dug out her phone gain. "Here I'm sending you the photos I took, just in case."

"Thanks. Quick thinking."

Evelyn winked. "I pick up a lot from those mystery novels and crime shows. But back at you thinking of the lost coupons."

Wanda chuckled. "We make a good team."

About that time, Angie reappeared, this time with her apron on, and handed them each the coupon section.

Wanda thanked her. Then she laid a hand on the girl's arm. "You okay, honey? Have you been crying?"

Angie's lip quivered. "It's nothing. Just a quarrel."

Evelyn stepped closer. "Well, I hope you and your boyfriend work things out. Sorry, I couldn't help but notice while I was searching for my coupons."

She scrunched her brow as if wondering what Evelyn talked about. Then her eyes lit. "Oh, no." She pointed down the street. "That was my, um, cousin."

She glanced away and whispered for the ladies to pardon her, but she had to get back to work.

"Cousin, my eye." Wanda tapped her foot. "Something has shaken that girl."

"Well, her brother did just become the area's latest murder victim. That would do it for me." Evelyn turned to retrieve her shopping cart. "You coming?"

"In a minute. I want to check on something."

"Okay. See ya."

Wanda walked over to the spot where the couple had their hushed conversation. Sure enough. A partial footprint had been stamped into the dirt next to the curb where the young man had stood. And a full print sat next to it, though the tread from the sole didn't appear as distinctive.

Even so, both seemed remarkably similar to the ones left near the church if her eyes didn't fool her. Wanda bent down, snapped a few pictures with her phone, and sent them along with Evelyn's to Todd with a text message. *Call me.*

He didn't. Okay, he could still be asleep. She'd give him time. In the meanwhile, she wanted to shop leisurely and watch the interaction of the grocery employees. A shudder in her gut told her one or more of these kids knew about the drugs.

As she passed by the bakery, Wanda saw Isaac huddled near Collin's office then slip away as she approached. The office door stood ajar, and Wanda heard two men's voices. One of them Collin's slight West Texas twang.

"I know these kids and their families. I cannot believe any of them would be involved with drugs or trafficking it."

The other man's voice held an even, professional, stern tone. Wanda couldn't make out his words because he spoke more quietly. Something about testing.

A chair screeched and slammed into something wooden, probably the desk. Footsteps clumped and Collin stood closer to the door, or so she surmised by the increased volume of his voice. "Fine. I'll comply though I cannot see how this will help. Here is the list of employees, including my own son. These six are here right now. Just be discreet. I don't want my customers unduly upset."

"We have to follow standardized procedures established by the Substance Abuse and Mental Health

Services Administration. Your restrooms will be closed to the public until all employees are tested. A lady officer will be present for female employees and a male for the men."

The door creaked open further, and Wanda slipped behind the display of cinnamon rolls and donuts. A man emerged whose demeanor and clothing choice screamed "Fed" to her. He talked on a Bluetooth giving the okay to set up for the drug testing.

Hushed voices filtered throughout the store as a team of lab techs weaved through the aisles with their equipment. Collin rubbed the back of his neck and mumbled something about it being all over town within the hour. And it would be, no doubt.

Wanda glanced around on tiptoes and noticed a raven-colored head slip through the double doors into the storeroom. On impulse, she followed her.

Suddenly the doors whammed behind her, making her almost jump out of her arch-reinforced loafers. "Customers are not allowed back here, Mrs. Warner."

She twisted around to find Miguel standing behind her, his arms pretzeled over his chest. Angie backed up and huddled near a stack of shrink-wrapped cereal boxes on a pallet next to boxes of canned vegetables.

"I um, was looking for the restroom."

"You passed by it. It's on the other side of these swing doors, as you well know." His eyes narrowed as his eyebrows almost met in the center of his face.

Think, fast. She gulped. “Yes, but those are being barricaded for some reason so I thought perhaps there might be one back here.” She scanned the room. “It’s kinda urgent.”

Angie stepped forward. “I’ll take her next door.” She hooked her elbow through Wanda’s and pulled her to the backdoor that led to the alley.

As they stepped into the sunlight, she noticed a white unmarked van parked near the dumpster. The same young man that she’d seen speaking to Angie leaned next to it.

Wanda’s heart thumped a few beats faster. Her women’s intuition told her she was not being escorted to a toilet after all.

Chapter Twenty-Seven

"My friend will wonder where I went. You know my nephew is a police officer. I am head of the neighborhood watch committee, and we are having a special meeting tonight. If I don't show up . . ." Wanda rattled off every excuse she could think of as Angie dragged her toward the van.

"Whatever. Get in."

The young man jerked the side door of the van open. "Do as she says, lady." He shoved her closer to the vehicle.

"Juan, no need to be rough on her. She's old." She took Wanda by the arm.

Old? Wanda let it go. At sixteen or seventeen most of the adult population would probably appear old. Anyway, she now knew the young man's name. Amateurs.

Wanda wrenched her arm away. "Okay. I will. Just give me a minute. I am not as spry as I used to be." She wobbled as she grabbed the door handle and hoisted herself up. As she did, she slipped her other hand in her slacks pocket and grasped a tissue she had used earlier in the day to blot her lipstick and discard her gum. As she pushed her leg up into the van, she dropped it near the wheel.

Lord, please let them not see it but let Evelyn or Todd notice it. They both knew she wore a deep rose-colored gloss and chewed peppermint sugarless gum.

Angie got inside with her, and the young man screeched the side door closed. Diffused light filtered through the dirty porthole windows in the back. It appeared as if butcher paper had been taped across them. Wanda crouched on the floorboard and Angie knelt opposite her.

"Kidnapping me is not the answer. It'll only get you in more trouble."

Angie cocked her head. "You got in willingly. I have a witness."

Right. The girl had some smarts.

The engine started with a few chugs and hacks, and Wanda smelled the diesel exhaust oozing up from the floorboards. It made her slightly queasy. Of course, not knowing what would happen to her in the next few minutes could have something to do with her change in disposition as well.

The young woman snatched Wanda's purse, took out her phone, and pocketed it. Then she slid the handbag to the back of the van. "Don't think of retrieving it."

My phone has a GPS tracker. Todd can find me. She

hoped neither Angie nor her "cousin" figured that out.

"I am sorry about your brother. He was in Shari's class, wasn't he?"

"Witch." Angie sniffled. "He never should have gone out with her again. If he hadn't, he might still be . . ." She swallowed the rest of her sentence in a gulp.

"Alive." Wanda tried hard not to react. "You think Shari got him involved in trafficking drugs hidden in the produce?"

Angie pushed Wanda in the chest. Her voice grew angry. "Yeah, and when he wouldn't play along, they killed him."

"Who are 'they'?"

"The same people who planted this in my grocer apron pocket to arouse suspicion." She pulled out a small baggie with white powder in it. "Make it look like one of us is doing this stuff so Shari and they can keep on making their contacts." She shoved it back into her apron and ran her hand under her nose. "I figured it out, and now they are after me, too. And she is orchestrating it all from her so-called sick bed, pretending she is more injured than she really is. I hate her."

Tears began to trickle down her cheek. She brushed them away and tossed her hair back.

"So where do I fit in?"

The van hit a deep pothole, which made Angie and Wanda both wobble.

It must be the one near 3rd Street and Ash where old Mr. Baker lived. This wasn't the best part of town, and the roads either ended in brushland or deteriorated into private graveled ones meandering toward hunting cabins amidst the scrub oak and mesquite woods east of town. Could that be where they were taking her? An abandoned cabin?

"Just hush, okay?"

Angie screwed in her listening device and scooted away, most likely to talk with her cousin, or whoever he really was, chauffeuring them. Her voice droned quietly though Wanda couldn't pick up all the words over the hum of the engine in definite need of a tune up.

Watching the girl's expression, she got a sense that the two truly were amateurs making this up as they went along. In over their heads, no doubt. Perhaps she could play that to her advantage.

In the meantime, she would have to stay alert and yet be as compliant as possible. Maybe gain Angie's trust. Afterall, she was only a teenager engulfed in something too large for her to handle.

Wanda waited for her to finish her conversation, then spoke. "Angie, I have a daughter who has been in and out of drug rehabs most of her life. I wanted to believe Shari had turned her life around, but I also know lying is another habit they take on. If you have proof that she is involved in this, give it to me. I promise to take it to my nephew."

Angie tucked her lip in her teeth. The van rocked again,

and the wheels' noises changed. From the pops and grinds, Wanda figured they had left asphalt and moved onto gravel. Through the opaque windows she saw shadows of tree limbs. Their journey became bumpier. That only meant one thing.

They were no longer in Scrub Oak.

How far did Todd's courtesy jurisdiction extend? Would he even be able to rescue her now? A hollow in the pit of her stomach grew into a worry wedge.

Get it together. God is with you. He will give you wisdom. No matter what happens, He already knows about it. A Scripture verse she had memorized from Bible study floated to the surface.

"God is our refuge and strength. Our very present help in time of trouble."[1]

David had written it hiding out in a cave from his enemies. Now, through the millennia, it reached out to her just as it, no doubt, had done to those being dragged into Babylon, or first century believers cowering from lion roars, or men in trenches hiding from cannon balls, or maybe sailors huddled in submarines dodging exploding depth detectors.

"Angie. Tell me what you know. I can protect you. You know I have influence."

The girl's eyes became wild with fear. "This isn't mine." She stood and began to jerk open the door to toss it.

---

[1] Psalm 46:1

"Wait. That's evidence."

She clutched it in her hand. "I don't want it to convict me."

Wanda struggled to her feet as the van continued to bobble over the uneven road. "Then let it convict someone else. There may be prints on it. DNA. You never know. It may be exactly what the authorities need to exonerate you."

"Really?" She slid to her behind, knees tucked to her chest.

"Just turn around. Let's go back. The authorities are testing employees. Show them the bag. Tell them you found it in your apron when you put it on today. Let them test you and see you're clean."

She spoke through her earpiece to the driver. The van screeched to a halt. Wanda listened as footsteps crunched the gravel and then the side door screeched open.

The light from the sun temporarily blinded her. She raised her arm over her eyes to shield them from the rays.

"Okay, lady. Talk to us."

She again laid out her argument.

"Juan, she makes sense. Let's go back."

He took Angie's hand in his and caressed her cheek.

Wanda saw tenderness in his eyes. He deeply cared for Angie. She decided these were good kids, simply scared.

Angie's eyes glistened. "I want to go to Eduardo's funeral. I want to tell him goodbye."

He brushed her lips with his. "Fair enough." Then he

turned to Wanda. “You better make good of this.”

Wanda shrugged. “Of what? After all I willingly got in the van, right?”

She winked at Angie and for the first time saw her face ease into a smile.

Chapter Twenty-Eight

The three drove back into town. Following Wanda's instructions, they stopped at Ash and 9th Street. Angie collected Wanda's handbag and returned it to her along with her phone. Juan left them there and went home, or so Wanda guessed.

Grateful to have her phone back, Wanda wasn't about to use it at this point. She and Angie walked to Red Bud Way and up through the alley.

"Do you still have to use a restroom?"

Wanda chuckled. "Not really."

Angie grinned. "What were you doing in the storeroom?"

"Following you. Something told me you were in trouble. My friend and I had seen you two talking earlier. You seemed upset. I wanted to help."

Angie squinted against the sun as she peered into Wanda's face. "People call you a busy body, don't they?"

Wanda sighed. Would she ever outlive that title? "I care about this town and its citizens. If we can't be there for each other who will?"

"Well, I don't think you are one. You're just a very nice lady." Angie stopped and sat on the curb. "I am so scared."

"Don't be. I will be right with you. I'm on your side. Just tell me why you think Shari is involved?"

They both glanced at a bus filled with small kids singing "Row, Row, Row Your Boat" as it passed by them on the side street. Must be on a field trip. How innocent the world must seem to them.

Angie waited until they passed then answered Wanda's question. "Adds up. She was into it in high school when they dated. Left a joint in his car for heaven sakes. I remember him coming into my room after he tossed it in the lake and hugging me so close it scared me. He told me if the police came, he needed me to understand he was innocent no matter what. I'll never forget that night. I woke at every sound. He was jumpy for a good week after that."

She swallowed and took in a shaky breath. "Two nights before he died, he came to my room and asked if I recalled that night. He told me it might be happening again. When the police banged on our door, I expected them to ask us where he was, not that he was, was . . ."

She turned and looked at the asphalt as tears trickled down her cheek. "If not her then who? And now she and her friends are trying to frame me as well."

"You don't know that. It could be anyone at the Grocery Mart. Maybe someone who was also trying to frame her."

The girl shook her head back and forth in rapid succession. "I can't do this." She bolted to her feet, tossed the baggie in the public trash can hanging on the traffic pole at the corner, and began to run.

Wanda tried to follow her, calling her name.

But the girl was forty-six years younger. And faster.

Wanda collapsed onto a bench outside of Anna's Antiques, out of breath, and prayed.

Chapter Twenty-Nine

Wanda heard the tinkle of a bell and then Beverly Newby's voice. "Wanda, dear. Are you all right?"

The older lady grabbed both of her hands and helped her up. But Wanda's knees became like gelatin.

"Come into the shop and I will get you a glass of water."

Wanda, with her hand pressed to her thudding heart, nodded, and let the woman help her inside to sit on a divan. In a minute, a glass of cool water was placed in her trembling hands. She took a sip, then another. Her heart still pounded as if a beginning drum student tried to find the beat to the song but couldn't quite get it. Her ears filled with humming, and she felt faint.

She vaguely heard Beverly call 9-1-1 as the room began to spin and a sharp, heavy ache in her chest pressed into her shoulder. The next ten minutes filled with sounds, sirens, and flashing lights. Men pressed on her, asked her questions, and hooked her up to leads. An oxygen mask covered her nose and mouth and the medicinal a taste of O2 whooshed over her tongue.

Wanda tried to protest but the men lifted her on a gurney and wheeled her backwards into yet another van, the second time today without her permission. This one had medical markings, thank goodness.

They continued to poke and prod her, asking questions—could she hear them, could she breathe, could she see the pin light, who was president—as the vehicle bumped and jolted to the Medical Center.

Then the van doors opened, and she was pulled into the sunshine feet first. She thumped, thumped in the gurney down to the asphalt and was wheeled, headfirst inside to fluorescent lights and ceiling tiles zipping by. Through swishing doors, voices jabbered rapidly as if in a foreign language. She heard the thunking of another door as they wheeled her into a small room and then lifted her limp body onto a bed. Medical staff buzzed around her like flies over a half-eaten drumstick at a picnic.

She gave in, closed her eyes, and let them do whatever they intended to do. Slowly the pressure on her chest eased as the invisible elephant moved away. Weariness won out and she drifted off to sleep.

Chapter Thirty

Wanda woke to beeps and a cold, white ceiling. It took her a moment to recall her surroundings. Hospital. Right.

"Hey, you're awake."

Todd's voice echoed in her brain, and she slowly turned her head in the direction of the sound. He grasped her hand.

"You're okay. They thought you might have been having a heart attack, but it seems you simply overstressed your body. What were you doing?"

She reached through the fuzziness in her mind. "Long story. Bear with me." She took in a breath.

"Take your time."

"I was running after Angie Espinoza. She became really upset. Someone put a small bag of drugs in her grocer apron pocket. She didn't know what to do and panicked."

"Okay?"

Wanda edged toward the guard rail, using it to pull herself to her side so she could gaze directly into Todd's eyes. "It seems Eduardo dated Shari in high school, and she left drugs in his car. He threw them in the lake but was freaked out, convinced the police would find out and arrest him. Angie remembers how upset he was. She said he began acting the same way when Shari showed up again."

"She thinks Shari tried to drag him into trafficking drugs?"

"I guess so." Why did she feel so tired? She fought to keep her eyelids open.

"Where is that bag of drugs now?"

"In the public trash bin tied to the traffic pole at Red Bud and Ash." She struggled against the drowsiness and lifted her hand. "I believe her, Todd. She was really, really scared."

He sighed through his nostrils and sat back. "And you got involved because . . ."

"I noticed her talking to her boyfriend around the corner from the Grocery Mart. She started crying. I guess the mother in me emerged." When she tried to raise herself off the mattress, the beeping increased in rhythm.

Todd glanced at it. "You need to rest. Thanks for letting me know. They are keeping you here for observation. Just in case. Seems your lab work was off kilter. They may run some more tests." He leaned in and kissed her cheek. "So, behave, okay?"

Wanda smiled and crossed her chest with her finger. What else could she do with all these wires attached to her?

"Todd, Go easy on her, please?"

"Yeah. I'll be a pussy cat. Promise."

Wanda envisioned him in the Broadway production of Cats as a young, striped tabby with a shiny coat but muscular and ready to pounce. It made her giggle. What drugs did they have her on anyway?

He gave her a curious stare. "What?"

"Never mind." She waved a hand in his direction. "Thanks for being here. Sorry if I scared you."

He winked. "I forgive you. This time." Then he went to the door. "I'll drop by later."

Later. The captain's meeting. She doubted they would let her conduct it in here. Oh, well, most of the town probably already knew of her hospitalization.

There was a nurse buzzer at her side, but no landline phone that she could see. Only a little table next to her with her purse.

And her phone. Eureka.

She spent the next fifteen minutes composing a text to send to each of them as she tried to focus on the small phone screen.

Then Wanda texted Evelyn to call her back. *I can't tell Todd, not yet. But I want to tell you what happened to me and why I briefly disappeared.*

Ten seconds later her phone rang. Good old Ev. Wanda explained the whole thing to her.

"Wow. No wonder your body got overstressed. I'm

sorry, I panicked when I couldn't find you. Miguel said Angie took you to find a bathroom. But neither of you returned."

"Panicked? What do you mean?"

"Didn't Todd tell you? I called him. Right after I saw an unmarked white van leaving the alley in a hurry. Something told me you were inside of it. Guess I was right."

Oh, great. And now Todd knew she had withheld evidence.

Chapter Thirty-One

Hazel Perks arrived with a small bowl of her prize-winning roses.

"When I was at A Cut Above for my monthly manicure . . . tending roses really damages my cuticles, the price one pays for raising beauties such as these . . ." she set the bowl on Wanda's bedside tray. "Anyway, I ran into Emma Mae Buckley who bopped in for some more shampoo. She had heard about you from Kathy King who heard through Beverly, Kathy's mother. My dear. How are you feeling?"

Small towns. Gotta love them. Wanda smiled and mumbled that she felt much better and thanked her friend.

Hazel hadn't been gone for two minutes before Betty Sue waltzed in, teary-eyed. "I thought I might lose my best friend."

To keep the emotions at bay, Wanda took a large gulp of water from the flimsy plastic cup the nurse had given her.

"I am so sorry I scared you and everyone else. I guess I need to step up my walking regime . . . no pun intended. Well, maybe it was."

Betty Sue giggled. "Now I know you're all right."

She leaned over and hugged her, filling Wanda's nose with her lavender scent. Then she straightened up, hands on hips. "What on earth happened?"

"I ran too fast and too far trying to catch up to a teenager in distress. I feared she might do something stupid . . ."

"Oh, dear. You mean end her life?"

"No. No. Have a seat." Wanda told her the whole story.

Betty Sue listened, her hands on her knees and her eyes occasionally widening. "You poor thing. No wonder you nearly keeled over. I would have been frightened out of my skin."

Wanda drained her water cup. "When I realized Angie's expression of fear mimicked my own, I knew I could talk her into not kidnapping me. But mind you, I did pray an awful lot."

Betty Sue rose. She took the cup and refilled it from the plastic, styrofoam-coated pitcher then set it back on Wanda's tray. "You can have more, right? I figured so or they wouldn't leave the pitcher in here."

"No one said I couldn't."

A tap on the door interrupted her. Now who?

A young man in scrubs entered. His shirt had *Dr.*

Young, Cardiology embroidered on it. Yes, he definitely was what his scrubs stated. *Young*. What had he done? Graduate from college at thirteen? Wanda almost asked him for his vitae curriculum.

"Mrs. Warner?" He glanced at her.

Wanda raised her hand. "Present."

Betty Sue swatted at her.

Dr. Young chuckled. "I want to go over your test results. Your Troponin T is slightly elevated. That may be hereditary. But your BNP is normal. That's good news." He pressed a button to raise her to more of a sitting position.

"In English, doc?"

He nodded and laid an iPad beside her. "I gather you've never had a cardiological work up?"

She shook her head.

He shifted his focus to Betty Sue.

"Oh, this is Mrs. Simpson, my dearest and oldest friend. Whatever you have to say can be said in her presence."

The young physician shifted his weight. He spent the next fifteen minutes proving his worth by explaining about enzymes and hormones, and valves, and arteries. At the end of his spiel, Wanda felt she could graduate from Med School, but she had to admit he did a good job communicating at her level.

"Bottom line is you're fine . . . for now. I would like you to make an appointment to have a complete work up in about three weeks. You should expect to be there for at least four hours."

Wanda blanched. How much would that cost? "Can I wait a few more years until I'm on Medicare?"

He smiled and mouthed a *no* as he handed her his business card. "My south office is only about a twenty-minute drive, so you don't have to trek all the way into Fort Worth. My office manager can go over the costs with you and arrange for payment options. She is better at that than I am."

He turned to leave. "I am discharging you tomorrow on one condition. Bed rest for two more days. Then pamper yourself for the next few weeks. Catch up on your to-be-read list or binge watch TV. Eat sensibly and take a half-hour stroll each day. Avoid stress as much as possible. No strenuous housework and no vigorous exercises until you have the new tests that I want done. Got it?"

She felt like saluting him, but instead she only bobbed her head up and down.

He gave her the smile they must practice in Med School because they all used it. It conveyed, *I am trying to show you I care, and you can trust me, but I must remain objective.* He exited, leaving the door wedged open.

Sounds of conversations, carts being wheeled, and machines beeping filtered in from the hallway. What time was it anyway?

"Well?" Betty Sue arched an eyebrow.

"I have my marching orders."

"I am at your beck and call. I can do your housework, laundry . . ."

Wanda raised her hands in front of her. "Whoa, Betty Sue? That's sweet of you, but no. I got some mad cash for my birthday last month. I'll hire one of those maid services. I think Hazel uses one."

"Yes. Clean Machine. In the four years she has had them, they have never broken any of her collectibles. I heard her say so."

That cinched it. Hazel Perks had more doo-dads, dust-catchers, and tchotchkes than anyone Wanda had ever known. Wanda may be a lady of leisure for a few weeks, but she didn't plan to lay off this case. Thanks to texts, social media, and cell phones, as well as her good friends as gofers, she'd figure this one out.

She only hoped Todd had found Angie safe and sound.

"Betty Sue. Do me a favor. You and Fred find out what you can about Angie and her boyfriend named Juan something. Poll some kids you know, and their teachers. I'm going to see what their social media footprints reveal."

"Do you think they are honest kids mixed up in something they don't know how to handle?"

"I hope so. Angie is very angry about her brother. Angry enough to point a finger at Shari and try to make her responsible. See if you can get a copy of her handwriting. They still handwrite things in school, don't they?"

Betty Sue giggled. “Yes, occasionally. Ah, you want to compare hers to the graffiti, right?”

Wanda winked. “Bingo.”

They heard a tap on the door as an aide entered with a tray. She smiled, set it down, and raised the lid. “Bon Appetit.”

The aroma of overcooked veggies and a rubbery semblance of a chicken breast with stamped-in blackened grill marks assaulted Wanda’s nostrils. No roll, no mashed potatoes. No butter. A green salad with vinegar and oil packets sat off to the left along with some iced tea, obviously unsweetened. Green gelatin cubes wiggled in a clear plastic bowl for dessert.

“Glad I had that big spaghetti squash lunch.” Wanda whispered it under her breath as she smiled at the retreating aide and unfolded the paper napkin.

Betty Sue shuddered. “I better leave you to it.” Then she added in a sing-song tone as she exited, “Be a good patient and gobble it down.”

Wanda forked some of the chicken, sniffed it, and groaned.

Chapter Thirty-Two

Wanda had never been so glad to see her living room the next day. Her easy chair in a soft turquoise, seafoam green and pink paisley angled toward her comfy pastel green sofa accented with turquoise, tan, and pink throw pillows she'd needlepointed in a wavy pattern when she was pregnant with her daughter. Was it really thirty-four years ago? Her flatscreen TV, a luxury present to herself when she retired, sat on the opposite wall in front of the double-paned window that looked out onto the front yard. Placing it there reduced the glare and also served the purpose of studying neighbors walking by when they thought she simply watched a show.

White bookcases flanked the fireplace with Tudor-styled diamond-paned windows above them. Photos, a brass candlestick with a turquoise candle, and a vase with fake carnations cluttered the mantle alongside a chiming clock. She wandered to the pictures and raised her hand to run her finger over the frames of each. Her late husband, Big Bill, grinned back at her in his fishing hat, holding up a wide-mouthed bass. B.J., her son, stood straight as an arrow in his Eagle scouting uniform, and Wesley, probably about eight, perched on a swing. Almost prophetic.

She could hear the shrill giggly voice now. "Higher, Mommy. Get me higher." Always seeking a thrill. Who knew her life would have so many back and forth, up and down moments? God did and that gave Wanda a small inking of hope.

"You okay?" Evelyn stood in the archway separating the living area from the dining room with Hazel's bowl of roses in her hand. She had driven Wanda home from the Medical Center.

"Yeah." Wanda sat in the chair, hands on her knees. "I had quite a scare, though."

"Saw your life flash before your eyes?" Evelyn entered, placed the bowl on the coffee table, and eased onto the sofa.

"Not quite. But it did hit me that we aren't getting any younger, are we? To be honest, we have more years behind us than we do in front of us."

Her neighbor sighed. "Thanks for the reminder."

After an awkward moment of silence other than the ticks of the clock and the clink of Sophie's tags on her collar as she scratched her flank, Wanda slapped her leg. "Well, I'm going to have a nice long soak in a hot bath, get into my robe, and veg out on old movies."

"Good girl. Can I bring you lunch? I guess a cheeseburger and onion rings is not an option but how about a chef salad from Sally's?"

"Um, make it a bowl of vegetable soup and a garden salad with low-cal ranch." Wanda reached for her purse. "And a whole wheat roll. I need some carbs in my life."

Evelyn held up her hand. "Uh-uh. My treat. No arguments." She rose and left by the backdoor.

Wanda soaked in the tub, with Sophie's chin resting on the rim, her mournful brown eyes boring into her master. She patted her pooch's velvety head. "I'm fine, girl."

As if satisfied, the dog sniffed and padded down the hall, most likely to her bed in the kitchen. Wanda chuckled and leaned back on her scalloped neck pillow.

Shari's face entered her mind. She wanted to believe the girl had truly found Jesus and turned over a new leaf, but why did she have a niggling that she hadn't? Did her own experiences with Wesley cloud her judgement?

"I did, did I?" It is as if Shari spoke out, daring them to prove it, and almost denying any involvement in drugs.

Angie sure held a grudge. Her brother's death of course had a lot to do with her emotional state. Even so, Wanda could not see her framing Shari. However, why else would she talk about someone putting a bag of dope in her apron?

Wait. That happened while Shari recovered at home. Did that mean Shari had an accomplice at the Grocery Mart? It had to be that way if Angie didn't lie. Either that or someone else besides Angie held a grudge and therefore wanted to frame Shari.

"She's only been here two days . . ." The angry voice of Miguel to Collin in his office floated to the forefront of Wanda's mind. She made a mental note to investigate that boy's past a bit deeper. Surf his social media links. Did he know Eduardo? Did the Garza family go to St. Joe's as well?

Her fingers started to prune so she flipped the drain stopper with her big toe and eased herself out of the still-warm water, which took longer than she expected. Maybe a bath hadn't been such a great idea.

Drying off and slipping into her fleece robe she padded down the hall and grabbed her note pad from the bedside table to write these things down before they evaporated from her slightly foggy mind. She always kept a notepad there in case a brilliant idea hit her in the middle of the night. Right now, she could use one.

But her eyelids felt like someone had sewn fishing weights from Big Bill's tackle box on them. Those new meds must be messing with her. She yawned, pulled up the afghan throw at the foot of the bed and curled onto her side.

Chapter Thirty-Three

A voice penetrated her dreams, though Wanda couldn't recall what they were. Betty Sue and Evelyn stood over her.

"Wanda, dear. You all right?"

Betty Sue's soft melodic voice lured her back to reality. She stretched and sat up as her two friends maneuvered pillows behind her for support.

I brought your lunch." Evelyn laid a tray on her lap.

"I brought you a handwriting sample from Angie." Betty Sue waved a piece of paper in the air. "And a jar of homemade loaded potato, cheese and broccoli along with some homemade croutons. You can eat it later on."

"Give me, give me." Wanda meant the paper of course. "So, Angie is all right?"

"Yes. She returned to the Grocery Mart today, telling Collin she just became overwhelmed with grief yesterday and had to leave. He told her he was not mad, just concerned. I overheard them as I picked out some mandarin oranges."

Good, Todd must have spoken to her. "And my phone. Where is that thing?"

Evelyn examined every surface in the room while Betty Sue dashed from the room, most likely to search the front of the house.

Then Betty Sue called out. "Found it. In her purse on the sofa." She hustled back down the hall and handed it to Wanda like a runner passing the baton.

Wanda thunked her head. "Stupid me. I printed them out, didn't I? Evelyn, can you go get the red folder on my desk?"

"Sure thing. Eat your vegetable soup before it gets cold."

With a nod, Wanda stirred it with her spoon and slurped some into her mouth. It did taste marvelous. She wrote on her pad to call and thank Sally.

Evelyn returned and opened the folder containing the photos of the graffiti. Wanda had paperclipped the female handwritings together, so Evelyn pulled out that stack and laid it next to Wanda's lunch tray.

Wanda eyed the photos and then the sample of Angie's handwriting. With a deep sigh, she tossed both on the bed. "Drat. No match as far as I can tell."

Betty Sue picked them up. Both she and Evelyn stared at them a minute then agreed. Angie's scrawl in no way resembled the graffiti artist's scribble.

"Now what?" Evelyn studied Wanda's face.

"We need to get handwriting samples of Miguel Garza's, Isaac's, and also of Eduardo Espinoza's, if possible. Perhaps Eduardo had to keep a log of his deliveries, or had to sign off on them at the Grocery Mart. Do you two think you can do that for me?"

"Yes, ma'am." Like good little soldiers, her friends replied in unison, saluted her, and then snickered.

Wanda smiled. "Good. Thanks. I'm going to eat lunch and go back to sleep."

If all the unresolved clues whirling inside her brain would let her. She wished she could shake them all out and examine them. Then, perhaps, she could solve this thing. Would Todd think it weird of her to have a whiteboard installed in her bedroom?

Probably.

Loaded Broccoli, Cheese and Potato Soup

This Potato Soup is so full of flavor and thick it seems more like a chowder! Perfect for those cold winter nights. Yes, it does dip into the low thirties in North Texas, and for us, that is cold!

Ingredients:

- 2 - 14.5 oz. cans chicken broth – Or you can use chicken bone broth.
- 2-3 large carrots, peeled and diced
- 4 medium potatoes, peeled and cubed into small pieces
- 1 tsp. onion powder
- 2 small heads broccoli, washed and diced small
- 3 Tbsp butter
- ⅓ c. flour
- 3½ - 4 c. milk
- 4 c. shredded cheddar cheese
- 1 tsp. salt
- ½ tsp. garlic powder
- ¼ tsp. pepper
- 6 slices bacon, cooked and chopped

Directions:

1. Combine the chicken broth, carrots, potatoes, and onion powder in a large pot. I use my mother's old stew pot with two handles. Bring to a boil, then cover and simmer for about 10 minutes.
2. Add broccoli, and then cover it again to simmer for another ten minutes.
3. While that is simmering, make a roux by melting butter in a large saucepan. Whisk in the flour and cook for another minute (or until golden brown). Whisk in milk and cook for an additional 5 minutes until the sauce thickens. Stirring constantly with the whisk keeps it from sticking or burning. Add cheese and stir until it is all melted then add the salt, garlic powder, and pepper.
4. Pour the cheese sauce into the large pot of

vegetables that is simmering and stir until well combined.

5. Add more milk for a thinner consistency if you like a thinner soup and add any additional salt and pepper as needed.
6. Top with crisp bacon crumbles and serve warm.

Great with slices of French garlic bread or homemade croutons.

Serves: 8-10

Chapter Thirty-Four

When she opened her eyes, Wanda saw the silhouette of a man sitting on her bed. The setting sunlight streamed through her bedroom window, outlining his form in golds and purples.

"Are you Todd or an angel coming to take me home?"

"Don't be overdramatic." Her nephew scoffed and repositioned his hip. As he did, it made her mattress dip.

"Aren't you supposed to be on shift about now?"

He raised his sleeve to check his watch, though she figured he already knew the time. "Got a few minutes. You up to chatting?"

"Sure." She grunted as she scooted further up on the bed and jammed the pillow behind her neck. "Did you find Angie?"

He laughed. "Now I know you're fine. Yes, I did. She ended up by the lake, crying."

"I wonder how long it took her to get there on foot?"

Wanda repositioned her shoulder. "That girl can run fast."

"Hmm." He knitted his brow as if trying to work it out in his head. "Anyway, I told her I knew she'd spoken with you, and you told me you were worried about her."

"Did she fess up?"

He exhaled a lengthy breath. "Yeah. But if you don't want to press charges, I won't arrest her and her boyfriend. Not on the eve of her brother's funeral. I'm not an ogre."

"She really hates Shari."

Todd rubbed his eyebrow. "I kinda got that impression. Blames her for Eduardo's death. And the fact the agents were investigating his past made her skin crawl, that is until I explained the process. Then she began to realize the necessity of tracing who in his life may have done this. It obviously wasn't Shari."

"Because from half-past-six on that morning she had witnesses to her whereabouts."

"Right, which is about the time of death, give or take an hour, per forensics. And the day before the grand opening at the grocers, Priscilla stayed with her to help her move in. She spent the night there. Shari was never alone for a good 20 hours before her assault." He pushed up from the bed. "Angie believes Shari's suppliers did it because her brother wouldn't cooperate."

"Is that the angle y'all are following?" Wanda hoped not, but it seemed the most likely.

"Honestly, Aunt Wanda, I don't think Shari is

responsible for any of this. The more I think about it the more I am convinced someone is trying awfully hard to frame her."

"Seriously? I thought being framed only happened on TV."

He leaned down and whispered in her ear. "She isn't Wesley."

A tear threatened as Wanda nodded. "Then prove it. I'm counting on you."

"Yes, ma'am." As Todd kissed her cheek, the scent of his aftershave warmed her heart but saddened it as well. She loved how their relationship had grown into a friendship, as it should with adult kids, but it seemed only yesterday he smelled of little boy sweat and bubble gum. Where had the time gone?

He straightened his spine. "Let's skip our game of Scrabble this week, just in case. Okay?" Then he winked and waved goodbye.

That is when she noticed the spring bouquet perched on her dresser. The sweet fragrance of the star lilies, mingled with the fresh smell of the daisies and baby's breath, whiffed toward her. Wonderful boy. "Todd?"

His footsteps halted in the hall. "Yeah?"

"They're gorgeous. Thanks."

"Welcome. Later."

She heard the faint sound of kibbles pouring into a bowl and the thump, thump of a wagging tail against the kitchen table leg. Then her backdoor clicked shut. *Bless him.* Some woman was going to appreciate him someday.

She started to roll out of bed. Afterall, she probably should feed herself.

Nah.

Wanda pulled the covers up, rolled onto her side, and closed her eyes again.

Chapter Thirty-Five

Her cell phone rang. Wanda swatted the bedside table for it and knocked it on the floor.

"Drat." She leaned over, her torso half off the edge of the bed to snatch it and answered, half out of breath as she scooched back onto the mattress.

"You okay?"

"Morning, Betty Sue. Yes. Just doing a few aerobics."

"Take it easy, dear. You know what the doctor said." Her voice sounded concerned. Then she became more chipper. "Well, we did it."

"Excuse me?" By this time, she'd wiggled herself to a sitting position and patted Sophie's head when she hopped up on the bed to join her.

"Well, almost. Evelyn retrieved Miguel's handwriting, clever woman. She pretended to not recall a brand name she liked and asked him to write it down for her, so she'd remember to buy it the next time she came into the grocers."

"Very nice."

"Uh, huh. And not just the brand name but the color of the box and the size, too."

Her feminine giggle trickled into Wanda's ear. It made her chuckle as well. "That'll definitely give us enough to compare."

"Yep, and I found Eduardo's. I went to visit Shari and started talking about him. She wanted to attend his funeral, but I talked her out of it. Anyway, I gently tugged her down memory lane, and she showed me her high school yearbook. He had written her a love note in it."

"Good thinking!"

"Thank you. I took a picture of it while she was in the restroom. But here is what is so weird."

"What?" Wanda felt fully awake now, even without her morning coffee.

"Priscilla came in, caught me looking at it, and blew a gasket."

"Because?"

She heard her friend sigh through the phone. "She told me Shari had been crying a lot over his death and how dare I dredge up bad memories. Then she yanked the book from my hands and walked out with it."

"Do you think she noticed you taking a picture, Betty Sue?"

"I'm not sure. But I think I've used up my welcome passes."

Wanda knew Betty Sue and Priscilla had become closer over the summer and she would never purposely bruise the reed of a budding friendship. Betty Sue had a heart as big as Dallas and it often became injured by people not as trusting as she.

"It'll be okay. I am sure emotions are running high over there right now."

"I guess. Anyway, I am sending it to your phone. We'll think of a way to get Isaac's."

"Ask Collin. Isaac is his son, so I'm sure he wants this resolved as much as anyone. Tell him it is for the purpose of elimination. In fact, get him to give you Angie's and everyone else's who works there as well, including Miguel so he doesn't become suspicious."

"Gotcha. I need to go get ready."

"For Zumba?"

"No . . ." Her word elongated in a stall. Then another sigh. "All right, but don't get all excited."

Well, that just fueled the flames. "Where are you going?"

"Fred has invited me to brunch at the Woods Grill."

Wanda bit her tongue to stop the squeal of delight from escaping. Instead, she took a breath and a sip of water, then kept her voice perfectly calm and steady. "Have fun. I hear their omelet buffet is amazing."

"That's what he said. You plate what you want to have in yours and the chef prepares it." She sounded excited, probably about more than the omelet. "Later."

Wanda heard a quick beep-beep on a phone. A photo of Eduardo's note to Shari appeared. Another set of beeps revealed another text from Evelyn with Miguel's.

Wanda studied each one of them for a few seconds. She set her phone down as a smirk spread over her lips.

Well, well.

Chapter Thirty-Six

Wanda texted Betty Sue. *Did Isaac, Eduardo, and Shari graduate together?*

I'll ask Fred. He kept a copy of every yearbook during his tenure as the principal.

But of course, he would. Who knew what other secrets those books revealed? She snapped her fingers, which jolted Sophie from a sound puppy dream.

"Sorry, girl. Your master is playing matchmaker." Her thumbs slid over her phone's keyboard. *Can y'all look through the ones during the time they were in high school and let me know if they all hung out?*

I'll ask him. Want us to bring them over?

Um, no. Three would be a crowd. *No, I may be napping. Just let me know if you discover anything interesting. Thx.*

Now that she'd sent the ball rolling down the alley, she hoped it would land a strike. Those two were meant for each other.

Eight-thirty. Todd would most likely be asleep. She'd bug him later. And until she knew the links between Shari, Eduardo, and Miguel, she didn't have enough to present him anyway. She'd have to wait until her friends did what she'd asked. Then she'd compile it and let him connect the dots.

Waiting had never been her strong suit. Neither was resting. Lessons God kept trying to teach her. She threw back the covers, whistled to Sophie, and headed to the kitchen to fix both of their breakfasts.

Opening the fridge, she noticed Betty Sue's jar of spaghetti sauce. Red. If it spilled it would resemble a crime scene. She giggled. Then it hit her, as things often do.

"Red rum, sir is murder." In other words, no matter how you looked at it, murder was murder. Eduardo's. But so was any crime. Like drug trafficking. Wrong never made a right. The artist had responded to the first one, "I did, did I?"

Did what? Murder Eduardo? Or hide the drugs in the veggies? *Think, Wanda think.*

She left her oatmeal whirring in the microwave, went into the living room to sit in her easy chair, and shut her eyes. She had been there that morning. How long of a time lapse existed from the time Shari heard the diesel engine and went out back to the time they heard her scream?

Wanda reached back into her memory and tried to replay it as if she rewound and watched a scene on DVD. Filter everything else out. Ignore the aroma of the oatmeal.

The beep of the microwave every 15 seconds to remind her to take it out. Sophie lapping at her water bowl. The cardinal calling for his mate outside the window. Someone's lawnmower humming.

Erase it all and go back in time. What had Priscilla said?

Shari had been upset about the late delivery and had been on the phone all morning. Then she'd heard the engine. Or so she said.

Then Shari had screamed. Priscilla and Sally had run out the back. How long had it been since Shari had exited? Long enough to possibly notice something else in the crates that did arrive.

Another question surfaced. Why only bring four? Why not scoop the rest in the other six crates and bring them as well? Answer—they didn't contain the drugs.

She wanted to see a photo of the scenes of the crash. Were the other six simply too damaged to bring, so the new driver brought what he or she could. Or did the new driver choose to deliver the four because those contained the hidden cocaine? Did Isaac or Miguel chunk the veggies to retrieve the white powder packets unnoticed? Did they use one of them to slip into Angie's apron?

If only the police had installed CCV in town. Then she could view the driver and perhaps pass his photo around to the neighborhood watch teams to see if anyone recognized him. All she had to go on was Shari's vague description, and that there had been two other people besides her in the alley. The driver and the person who whacked her in the head with a spray can.

But wouldn't the graffiti artist, if caught in the act, have run away as soon as the van pulled into the alley? Of course, he or she would have.

That was it. The thing that didn't make sense. The piece of the puzzle that refused to fit. Shari had either been mistaken or had lied. No way were there two others in that alley.

Think back.

Priscilla heard Shari scream and rushed out there. She and Sally had been on the back stoop when Wanda and Betty Sue arrived from the alley.

Where were the other employees? Isaac, Miguel, Angie?

Hold on. Angie knew her brother drove for the produce company Shari hired. Wouldn't she have been just as antsy about why he was so late in arriving?

No. She would have been in school at the time. Rule her out. But Isaac and Miguel had been there because they scrubbed the wall later.

No one saw the driver except Shari. She remained the only one who could identify him, and she kept being vague about it. Why? Due to the knock on her head or something else?

The county guys had called in the Drug Task Force

once drugs had been detected. Perhaps they knew more, but no way would she be able to get them to talk.

Wanda stared at the ceiling and let out a long, slow breath. Maybe she should give it up. Let the professionals solve the drugs, the crates, and Eduardo's death.

The thing is, she now knew who the guy was that had sprayed the graffiti for two and three. Now she needed to discern who the girl had been and how they were connected. Dollar to donuts all roads lead back to Shari, even if she was innocent.

Wanda still had her doubts.

The first graffiti palindrome had been sprayed by a girl. Would a girl have whacked Shari in the head? Doubtful, especially if the palindrome didn't have anything to do with the case.

No, they were connected. Had to be. Solve that and it would lead to solving Eduardo's killer.

But why palindromes?

Then she remembered. A drug dealer in Dallas used them as a code. Way too coincidental considering Dallas lay an hour up the road. How could she find out who he was without endangering herself and her friends?

Wanda decided to eat her oatmeal first. Her stomach growls interfered with her thought process. Oh yeah. She had never eaten dinner, had she? No wonder her tummy complained. She rose from her chair and padded back into the kitchen.

Once she finished breakfast, she called Tom Jacobs. After all she had promised to keep him informed. “Tell me about this drug dealer in Dallas who uses palindromes.”

“You don’t play around, do you? I heard you were in the hospital for overexertion. Not chasing after underworld lords. You weren’t, were you?”

“No, Tom. But I can’t help but think that these palindromes are somehow connected to drug trafficking and Shari’s attack.”

He paused. “Then you’ll want to know this. I think someone is on your trail.”

Her heart jerked. “Why?”

“A new one appeared on the walls of the Medical Center last night. They said, ‘Level madam, level.’”

Todd had not said a word. Nobody had. Were they all protecting her?

“Can you send me a picture?”

“On the way to your phone. I’ll email you links to articles on that dealer if you promise not to head to the Metroplex.”

“Promise. Thanks, Tom.”

“Wanda, take care. I mean it.”

“I plan to. Believe me.”

A few seconds later her phone beeped. Wanda pulled up the photo and sent it to her printer.

She rushed to the second bedroom and grabbed it as it came through the feeder. Wait a minute. Could it be?

Locating the folder of graffiti samples, she picked up two and three and compared them to this new one. Her eyes darted from one to another. No doubt about it. The same guy who painted number two and three made this new addition. So, the conversation continued.

But was it meant for her, or someone else . . . namely the female writer?

Wanda wished she knew.

Chapter Thirty-Seven

The articles Tom sent provided little information. The man seemed to be a shadow. Then again, weren't most of these moguls who dealt in the underworld of crime deeply hidden from public view? She hardly expected to find a picture of him in the society section.

From what the articles stated he must have a large territory throughout south and east Dallas. Some people called him "the Great Geek" and others "the Orator Chemist." Strange title for a drug lord. Guess it meant he obviously had smarts. But did his tentacles stretch as far southwest as to encompass Scrub Oak?

Wanda hoped not. However, someone's obviously did. Perhaps one of his underlings tried to break out on their own. If that was the case, they may end up being squashed like a bug on a windshield. A body would be found by a vacationer in one of area lakes, by a coyote rooting in the brush, or by a traveler changing a tire and seeing it dumped in a bar ditch like Eduardo's.

Wanda set the articles aside. She didn't want to get knee-deep in the drug investigation. Let the professionals delve into that. However, her toes already dangled in the muck because this had happened in her community.

But first she needed another short nap. She stretched out in her recliner and closed her eyes.

The mantle clock bonging pulled her out of a deep sleep. Eleven in the morning. Todd should be awake. She called him to tell him she knew the identity of one of the graffiti artists.

"You're sure?"

"Absolutely, though why he'd spray paint his dad's business is beyond me. However, Collin needs to know. Remember, Miguel talked to Collin about a female employee he wanted fired even though she'd only been there two days. Shari is the only one who fits that description. For some reason Miguel was out to get her."

"Don't you dare call Collin. Not yet. I'm coming over to get the photos of Miguel's handwriting. No offense but I want a professional to tell me the sample you have is identical to our artist's."

"Including the one on the wall of the Medical Center."

Silence. Todd's voice softened. "Ah, you know about that. I didn't tell you because the doc said you needed rest."

"Todd, did Miguel mean it for me or did he paint it because he knew I'd probably see it there on the way to the parking lot when I checked out? And I would have if Evelyn had not driven over to pick me up at the front entrance."

"If it is Miguel, I plan to ask him just that question. Promise me you will not confront him until the handwriting expert is consulted."

"Very well. Besides, it is only half the puzzle unless he knows who his counterpart is. And why they chose to communicate this way."

"You mean in such a public manner?"

Wanda stopped. Was her own nephew baiting her or had he not been informed? "No, in palindromes. Like the ones the Great Geek uses in Dallas."

His voice exploded. "Aunt Wanda, stop. Whatever you have your fingers in, pull them out. Now. I mean it."

Wanda's heartbeat thudded in her ears. Talk about role reversal. Now she felt like the child and he the parent who caught her hand in the cookie jar a half-hour before dinner. "I do read the papers, Todd."

His tone calmed. "Aunt Wanda. Eduardo's was a professional hit. No doubt about it." He metered his words, obviously to make sure she heard him and understood. "I know what Angie believes. And I have spoken again with Shari. I do not see her involvement in this. But she has elaborated her testimony."

"Oh?"

"She admits she noticed the drugs in the crate and yanked them from the vegetables. She waved a pack at the driver and asked him what it was all about. That is when someone attacked her."

"And she didn't tell you before because . . ."

"She feared if she came forward, she would be implicated again and sent back to jail. Shari told me she did use in high school but only a few times. She says Eduardo dealt and talked her into using. Not vice versa. But Eduardo's and Angie's testimonies trumped hers, so the judge believed them."

Wanda rolled her eyes. "And she got the raw deal. Yada yada. They all say it."

"Yes, but she has proof. The night she broke up with him she recorded it on her phone. She saved it on a drive and let me listen to it."

"She didn't present this to the judge six years ago?"

"He stated it was inadmissible. Which is not true since she was part of the conversation. One-party-consent is perfectly legal. But there you are."

Wanda gasped. "Then she could appeal. Say she was unfairly tried."

Todd sucked in his breath. "Exactly and Priscilla is pushing her to do it. She would still be found guilty of possession, just possibly not for distribution. Even though it is after the fact, it could make a difference to any future employers."

He paused again but Wanda could hear his quick breaths through the phone. Something agitated him. "Todd?

What is it?"

"I need you to back out, Aunt Wanda. Please. Someone killed Eduardo and this may partially be why."

"Because he knew the distributor?"

"Or he wasn't as innocent as everyone thought. This tape, were it to go public, might blow his cover. It wouldn't take long to connect the dots. Did you know they found over a thousand dollars inside sandwich bags taped to the underside of his box spring mattress?"

"Hush money?"

"We aren't sure. Could be payment for deliveries. Someone silenced him anyway. Either he got cold feet and threatened to squeal or—"

"—or the mastermind saw him as too much of a liability once he started trashing Shari again and went to Plan B."

"Yep." Todd gulped loud enough for her to hear. "Of course, there is another scenario. Revenge."

Her mind clicked like a camera set on automatic. She jumped to her feet. "Wait. You don't mean—? Not Shari. There is no way . . ."

"No, but she or her sisters could have hired someone. Perhaps Eduardo began to trash her name and point fingers at her again to deflect attention from the real person behind this scheme."

Wanda couldn't help it. A nervous laugh burst from her diaphragm. "We're talking about Sally and Priscilla.

Respected shop owners. Pillars of our community. Their mother taught you in Sunday school for goodness sakes."

"I know. Which is why they are looking into Shari's other connections. I can't go into further detail. Just promise me you will back off. You may know too much already."

Her head hurt, right above her eyebrows as if someone tightened a rubber band around her temples. She sat back down and took in several breaths.

"Aunt Wanda?"

"I'm here. Fine, I'll back down. I need to rest as the doc said anyway."

"Good girl."

"But Todd, Evelyn was to talk Collins into getting handwriting samples from all of the employees. Miguel is going to know we are on to him if he does."

He cursed. She almost reprimanded him over the phone for filling her ear with such language, but then he apologized.

"Sorry. That slipped out. Text Evelyn or call her. Tell her to stop. Let me know if she has actually talked with Collin or hasn't been able to yet."

"I will."

"Aunt Wanda. Get some rest. Stay safe. You scared the bejeebers out of me yesterday. I love you."

He hung up.

That hit her in the heart. She sniffled as she stared at her darkened phone screen. "I love you, too, boy. More than you could ever know."

At that moment she felt a deep urge to pray for Shari, Angie, Miguel, and whoever else this ugliness involved.

Who knew wordplays could be so dangerous?

Chapter Thirty-Eight

After she both texted and left a message on Evelyn's voice mail, Wanda decided to catch up on the online crossword puzzles from the Fort Worth newspaper. She tossed an afghan over her raised feet and adjusted the lamp on the table beside her. This would keep her mind busy. Maybe.

A knock sounded on her kitchen door and then Betty Sue's lilt called out a yoo-hoo.

"In the living room." She pushed the recliner's foot support down and set her laptop on the table next to her.

"Are you decent? Fred is with me."

Wanda smoothed her hair. Did she still have on any make up? Probably not. Would Fred care? Probably not. "I guess I am. Come on in, Fred."

The couple entered with a small stack of yearbooks. Betty Sue gracefully lowered herself to the floor and opened them onto the coffee table. Fred sat on the couch.

"These are from several years ago. You are correct, Wanda. Eduardo and Isaac did hang out together." She tapped the page that showed them in a group of boys holding black and white balls in front of a net. "They both played on the soccer team. But look what else we found."

She flipped to a page in the second album. There were Eduardo, Miguel, and a third boy with thick black glasses and a crew cut style. The caption read, "Debate team wins semifinals in State."

Wanda stared at the photo. "Eduardo Espinoza, Miguel Garza, and Dennis Alberts? Wow. Miguel seemed so much younger. I'd never guess he was Shari and Isaac's age. Not much younger than Todd."

She studied the photo again. Her hand went to her mouth. "The Great Geek. The Orator Chemist. Oh, my word. Dennis sinned."

"What?" Betty Sue glanced at Fred who shrugged and then focused back onto Wanda.

She grabbed her laptop and pulled up the article Tom had sent her. She told him about the Dallas drug lord who used palindromes to communicate.

"Are you saying these graffiti messages are a code for drug dealers?" Fred's expression paled.

Wanda shook her head. "I think it is still a dialog. There is a new one. Hold on." She rose and went to retrieve her folder from her bedroom. Then she returned and laid them out over the yearbooks.

"See, Fred. Some are in a masculine handwriting. Thanks to Evelyn we are fairly sure they are from Miguel. Todd is having them analyzed. The others resemble the penmanship of a girl."

"Do you know who?" Betty Sue's eyes widened.

"Not yet. At first, I thought of Angie but now I don't. One, she would have been in school, and two, these seems to be defending Shari. Something she would not do."

"I always tried to get as many of the graduating students as possible to sign these yearbooks. Of course, at the end of the year it is hard to grab them." Fred picked up the latest one. "Let me see if I have any from Shari." He scanned the pages. "Ah, here is one."

Wanda craned her head as he turned it toward her. She gazed at the photo of the first graffiti and then back to Shari's scrawl. "Similar. But perhaps not exact. See, the d is slightly different. Though from an angle, like crouched and spraying up . . ."

"If conked on the head, would you graffiti a wall?" Betty Sue shook her head. "Besides, Shari lay in a hospital bed or at home recouping from a mild concussion after that. No way would she have been able to paint these others."

"True." Wanda sat back and tapped her chin. "Then who did?"

Her two friends stared at her with blank faces.

"May I keep these, Fred? I want to see who else Shari hung out with in high school."

"Oh, I can tell you that." He turned several pages and pointed to one with three girls laughing by a set of lockers. "Becky Turner and Mary Lou Fitzgerald. They were on the pep squad and designed all the banners the sports teams ran through."

"Becky Turner. Her mother lives on Mulberry, right? In the red-brick Edwardian?"

"That's right. Becky is in my Zumba class. You know her." Betty Sue scooted forward now that all eyes were on her. "If I recall, Becky went to Baylor University. Majored in graphic design. She is employed by an advertising firm in Houston. She moved back here to take care of her mother after she became crippled from that horrid auto accident last fall. Works remotely now."

That sounded vaguely familiar, though Wanda didn't know the family very well. "And Mary Lou is our church organist. She also designs the bulletin boards for the various ministries. Surely she wouldn't . . ."

Wait a minute. Wanda jolted from her chair and hurried into her bedroom again. She began digging through some papers on her desk. It had to be there somewhere unless she threw it out. Aha. The calendar for the month showing when each group or ministry had booked the classrooms with a handwritten note asking about coffee for the captains' meeting.

Wanda carried it back to the living room where Betty Sue and Fred sat. She flattened out the folds and laid it on top of the yearbook opened to the three girls' photo. Then she set the first of the graffiti on one side and the fifth one with Dennis' name on it on the other side.

"Well, I be." Fred shook his head.

Betty Sue gasped and raised her eyes to Wanda's.

Wanda bobbed her head. "I better call Todd."

Chapter Thirty-Nine

Twenty minutes later he knocked on her backdoor and let himself in. A middle-aged man with scarecrow features entered timidly behind him.

"Aunt Wanda, Betty Sue, Principal Ballinger." Todd tipped his Stetson to each and then removed it and hung it on the peg near the front door.

"Please. Unless you want me to call you Officer Martin, it is Fred."

Todd blushed. "Yes, sir. Sorry. Old habit." He motioned to the mousy man standing next to him. The guy's expression held an awkwardness to it, not quite a shyness, more like feeling out of place.

"This is Mr. Malcom DeBeer. He is the handwriting expert for the Dallas police force. We met in Austin when I was in college. He's the brother of my professor in criminology and criminal psychology."

The man cleared his throat and pushed his thick, black-framed glasses back up onto the bridge of his nose. “Actually, I am a certified graphologist. I work as the Forensic Document Examiner.”

“Ah.” Fred smiled.

Wanda asked them if they wanted refreshments. Both declined. Todd grabbed two dining room chairs and was about to drag them into the living room.

“Wait. Let’s all sit in the dining room. The light is better, and we can spread things out.”

“Good idea, Aunt Wanda.” Todd, along with Fred, and Betty Sue, gathered the yearbooks, pictures of the graffiti, Miguel’s handwriting sample, and then Mary Lou’s.

Mr. DeBeer clicked open his briefcase and took out rulers, calipers, and what looked like a magnifying glass.

What next? A Sherlock Holmes pipe? Wanda stifled a giggle. Nerves, most likely. Patient anticipation was not one of her virtues.

Todd glared at her then sat down himself.

Fred pulled out a chair for Betty Sue and that act of chivalry made her the apples of her cheeks pink.

DeBeer held up the round, glass device. “We call this a measurement reticle.” He flashed them a miniscule grin and then bent to study the evidence.

For the next few minutes all remained as silent as a graduate student’s library except for the ticks of the mantle clock and Sophie’s soft snores in the kitchen. Occasionally, DeBeer grunted or made a sound with his lips pressed together.

Wanda tapped her foot under the table and tried not to stare at the little man with the balding spot like a Medieval monk.

At last, he sat back and nodded.

"Well?" It blasted from her lips before she knew her brain thought it.

Todd flashed her an exasperated expression and then turned to his friend. "What is your expert opinion, Malcolm?"

"No opinion, Todd. No, no, no. Calculated observation. I would say there is a ninety-two percent likelihood the young man who wrote this note also penned the second, third and sixth graffiti."

"He means Miguel, right?" Betty Sue turned to each of the others for confirmation.

"Yes, dear lady, if you are certain this Miguel wrote this note."

Wanda wiggled in her chair. "We are. Yes."

The graphologist cleared his throat and set those aside. "Now as for the more feminine handwriting, and I agree the remaining ones are most likely penned by a woman. The style indicates someone in her twenties. Handwritings, like popular idioms and music, vary from generation to generation. Adolescents are such copycats."

He scoffed, or was it a chuckle? Wanda couldn't tell. She jiggled her foot again. *Get to the point.*

Betty Sue glanced at her and gave her a soft smile.

Right, patience is a virtue. It seemed God was intent on teaching her that lesson.

He briefly eyed the samples again and then bobbed his head more firmly. "Seventy-four percent chance this Mary Lou is the author. Also, there is an ever so slight deviance in the ds between number one and number five, possibly meaning two different young women wrote them. If so, it is my opinion that they are very well acquainted and have been for a while. I say that because girls tend to mimic each other more than boys."

Todd sat back and whistled. "Who would have ever suspected?"

"The question remains, dear nephew. Why?"

He scratched his head. "Exactly what I plan to ask Mary Lou when I visit her. You want to tag along, Malcolm?"

His face showed some animation for the first time. "Actually, I rarely get to see an interrogation in action. Always work behind the scenes. It might be a noteworthy experience."

Wanda pressed her lips together to keep from smirking. As hostess she decided she should be the first to rise. Todd leapt to pull out her chair and Fred did the same for Betty Sue.

She walked them to the door and laid a hand on Todd's arm. "Keep me posted."

He placed his Stetson on his head. "I will." Then he

turned his focus to Fred and Betty Sue standing quite close together.

"Thanks, you two. Good work."

Betty Sue blushed even more. She wiped his thanks away with a swish of her hand. "It was all Wanda's idea."

Malcolm DeBeer bowed. "Very well done, madam."

He and Todd exited.

Wanda closed the door and leaned on it. "Well, what do you make of that?"

All three broke into laughter.

Fred raised his finger in the air. "Senior Sleuths unite. We'll show this community we are not ready to be put to pasture yet."

Wanda and Betty Sue responded in unison. "Hear, hear."

Chapter Forty

The next morning a light mist fell over Scrub Oak. Appropriate weather for a funeral. Todd arrived in his cruiser and parked it in front of Wanda's house.

She grabbed her umbrella and shuffled out to greet him.

"Well?"

"Not now. Let us pay our respects, then you can gather all your friends together around your dining room table and I will fill you in back here."

Patience again, ugh. But he was correct. Now was not the time, especially if it soiled Eduardo's name. Angie and his mother didn't need to learn about that today.

Evelyn met them at the curb. They took her car because it comfortably sat more than four. Todd drove at her suggestion, and they picked up Betty Sue and Fred.

Todd cocked an eyebrow when he noticed them walking together, Betty Sue's arm laced through Fred's elbow.

Evelyn leaned forward from the back seat to view through the windshield as the couple approached. “When did that happen?”

Wanda winked. “The seed has been germinating a while. It has just started to bud, I think.”

“Aunt Wanda?” Todd’s tone held a reprimand.

She blinked in innocence. “I had very little to do with it.”

“Uh, huh.” He pushed the button to unlock the back door for the two passengers. Evelyn scooted over to give them room.

They arrived at St. Joseph’s ten minutes before the service began but the parking lot had already filled. Todd circled the block and found a parking spot on the street half a block down.

As they scurried to the double doors of the sanctuary, Evelyn whispered in Wanda’s ear. “Are they gonna speak in Latin?”

“I’m not sure they do that anymore. Spanish, maybe.”

The church entrance demanded piety. Tall, mahogany arches and stained glassed windows depicting the life of Christ dwarfed the pews. At the far end sat an altar draped in white and gold embroidered fabric with candles flickering. Off to the side, an organ quietly played.

The small group from Scrub Oak followed the other mourners inside. Some stopped to dip their fingers into a water bowl and make the sign of the cross. Others dipped to their knees before entering a pew. Many of the women wore black lace scarves over their heads, including Angie and her mother as they filed into the front row.

Then the priest read from Scripture as they wheeled the casket down the center aisle.

Wanda found it all fascinating and very reverent. Especially when a robed man waved a brass container of incense over the casket and the altar. The aroma of frankincense, roses, and cinnamon billowed in the air and the veil of smokiness added a quiet, almost holy ambience to the church. It reminded her of a passage in the book of Revelation.

The whole service lasted about an hour. Then they all walked across the street to the church's cemetery for the burial. Wanda turned to her friends.

"Let's leave. It looks as if not everyone is going to attend the burial. We didn't really know them."

Todd leaned in. "I thought you wanted to observe the suspects like the detective do on TV."

She flashed him an exasperated silent message with her eyes.

He chuckled and motioned for them to head for the car. Evelyn, Betty Sue, and Fred followed.

No one spoke on the half-hour drive back to Wanda's.

The group filtered into her dining room as Wanda took drink orders, offering iced raspberry tea, coffee, or water. Betty Sue helped her plate some grapes, cheese, and crackers, then they all settled around the table for a brief prayer led by Fred.

The initial chatter of passing the food and making sure everyone had what they needed waned. Wanda focused on Todd.

"Well?"

He winked. "Deep subject."

She groaned.

Fred laughed. "You used to say that in high school, Todd. I remember it well."

Todd bit into a cracker topped with Gouda and then set it on his plate. He took his sweet time chewing. Wanda knew it was to play with her patience, which at that point was so thin one could see through it.

Finally, he swallowed. "Mary Lou confessed. She wrote the fourth and fifth one at Shari's request. Shari admitted to spraying the first one. Marvin stated anger or fear may have made her hand shake enough to alter her handwriting a tad bit." He stopped to take a sip from his coffee mug.

Wanda, Betty Sue, and Evelyn exchanged puzzled glances.

"Wait, Isaac said he saw the artist the second time at the grocers. He definitely told you it was a guy."

Todd crossed one leg over his knee and leaned into the back of the chair. "You heard that, huh? I knew he lied because the forensic handwriting expert had already surmised the opposite. I didn't know why but I do now." His lips oozed into a sheepish smirk.

Wanda knew he baited her. "Why?" She tossed a grape at his face and missed. It landed on his chest.

"She's his girlfriend's BFF. Along with Shari." Todd plucked the grape from his shirt.

"Aha. Of course." Fred chuckled. "Shari, Mary Lou, and Becky. They always hung out together in school."

Betty Sue's mouth formed a little O. "I'd forgotten all about that when we looked through the yearbooks. Isaac's been dating Becky for a few months now." Betty Sue wiggled her eyebrows. "Her mother has already picked out her wedding dress."

"I bet she has." Todd and Fred eyed each other and groaned. Then Todd continued. "But Shari definitely wrote the first one."

"When did she have time? The graffiti paint dripped fresh." Wanda lifted her hands in front of her and shrugged her shoulders.

Todd's demeanor returned to cop mode. "Shari finally 'fessed up after I spoke with Mary Lou. She told me she figured something had happened to Eduardo. He helped her haul in her things to her new apartment and told her he knew drugs were being transported in the veggies. To be careful in case there were some in her shipments. He knew who orchestrated the whole thing and that scared him, so he didn't want to squeal."

"The Great Geek." Wanda almost whispered it.

"Exactly. Eduardo told Shari he and Miguel had already cooperated on some deliveries and gotten paid some good cash. That explains the money we found hidden underneath his bedding. But he decided to stop when one of the Great Geek's underlings got word the Drug Force became suspicious. Miguel had the idea of pinning it on Shari, but Eduardo's conscience got the better of him."

Fred huffed. "He couldn't do it twice to her."

"Right. He told Miguel after the delivery he planned on coming to us and spilling the beans. And he paid for that with his life." Todd's eyes clouded for a moment. Then he took a breath and blinked. "When he didn't show up that Monday morning her anxiety level rose. She texted him several times asking him why the delay. Of course, we now know why he never responded."

Evelyn bowed her head. "God rest his soul."

Everyone sighed and lowered their eyes.

After moment, Todd resumed. "She got a text about fifteen minutes before the truck arrived. A palindrome. 'No lemon no melon.' She knew it was from the Great Geek or one of his men telling her to shut up and play along."

"And she freaked because she knew the police would suspect her first." Wanda crossed her arms over her chest.

"That's right, Aunt Wanda. When the new driver arrived, Shari said she figured it all out and confronted him. She picked up a paint can left in the alley after Isaac and

Miguel had made new signs for the windows and wrote out a message for the Great Geek letting him know." Todd popped a fresh grape in his mouth.

Wanda leaned back in her chair. "I did, did I?"

"Who whacked her?" Evelyn's brow crinkled.

He swallowed. "I'm guessing Miguel. She honestly doesn't know. Nor did she recognize the substitute deliverer. She has agreed to get with the Drug Task Force's forensic hypnotist to see if they can come up with an accurate depiction locked somewhere in her memory."

Evelyn straightened in her chair. "Oh, I know about this. I have seen them do it on TV. Then the hypnotist can take it to a sketch artist who can put it through the FBI database and see if there is a match."

"That's the plan." Todd tapped his temple. "Actually, we are going to let the Drug Force guys handle all of that."

"I'm glad she has 'fessed up now, even though when she was assaulted and found out about Eduardo, it seems to have tightened her lips even more." Evelyn huffed. "Can't blame her, really."

"We hope the judge will see it that way. Right now, we have to charge her with withholding information pertaining to a crime and possibly as an accessory. But since I convinced her to cooperate, I am hoping the authorities will take that into account and drop those charges."

"So how did Mary Lou get involved?" Betty Sue scanned everyone's faces for an answer.

"Priscilla and Shari convinced her to do it." Todd leaned forward, his elbows flat on the table and hands clutched. "Shari kept wanting to plead her case. She knew the palindromes would send the right message to the right person."

"Dennis Alberts." Wanda scoffed.

"Very good, Aunt Wanda." Todd winked at her, which made the pride in her heart rise. He then shifted his focus. "Thanks to your digging, Fred and Betty Sue, the Feds now believe they have identified the Great Geek to be Dennis. I imagine we will hear about it soon on the evening news."

"Speaking of news. Are you ever going to tell me what you and Tom were so secretive about?"

Todd blanched. "I can't ask you to drop that, can I? Okay, he wants to do a full-page tribute to you and the neighborhood watch captains. I'm not saying anything else." He motioned a zipper over his mouth.

Wanda felt the heat rise into her cheeks and eyes. She glanced down to pet Sophie to give herself time to compose herself again. But now that her emotions were on the table, she decided to apologize. Another hard lesson God had been teaching her. One would think at sixty-two she'd learned it by now. She raised up and sucked in His strength to coat her flip-floppily tummy.

"I need to make a public apology. I'm sorry I doubted Shari. You're right, Todd. My experiences with Wesley tainted my viewpoint. I plan to ask Shari's forgiveness. She gives me hope that one day Wesley will turn to Christ and turn over a new leaf. I wish her nothing but success."

Betty Sue gave her a side hug. "Good for you."

"She will appreciate you telling her, but don't dillydally." Todd raised his chin. "Collin will reopen the organic section next week, but Shari will not be running it. She's moving to Fort Worth."

"What?" The three women responded in unison.

"It seems Shari has been offered a purchasing position with a statewide organic grocery chain. They liked the idea of only dealing with the local growers closest to each of their stores' locations."

Todd stopped for a moment and took another long sip of his coffee. "By the way. We have a warrant out for Miguel to bring in as a person of interest in both the graffiti vandalism and the drug trafficking. He seems to have disappeared."

"Figures." Evelyn harumphed. "I never trusted that family."

Wanda suspected Evelyn's view was tainted by the fact she was not only a teetotaler but the first woman to be elected a deacon at the church across the street from the liquor store.

Todd moved on. "Obviously, he responded in palindromes at someone's request and given his history with Dennis, well . . ."

Wanda raised her finger. "And he and Eduardo did

transport drugs."

"Hearsay. We have no proof other than Shari's testimony."

"What about the palindrome text she got? Can you trace it to the sender?" Fred reached for another cracker and cheese slice. He plopped it in his mouth.

"Shari erased it. But Malcom knows of a few guys in Dallas forensics who can probably retrieve it. Again, that's for the Feds and Drug Task Force to handle."

"Level, madam, level." Wanda said it half under her breath. "Was that for me or Shari?"

"No telling, Aunt Wanda. But this Great Geek is well connected. You could have very well been watched. I admire your sleuthing skills and I know your intentions are honorable, but I do worry about you sometimes."

"And I worry about you, dear Todd. I always will."

He reached out and grasped her hands across the table. "Then my darling aunt, it appears that we will always have words between us."

She gulped back the tears.

It made usually stoic Evelyn's eyes shimmer as well.

Betty Sue took in a shaky breath and whispered to Fred, explaining the message's meaning scrawled in the high school dictionary Todd gave to Wanda upon graduation. "They've always loved playing word games together."

"In other words, they will always have each other." Fred patted her hand. "Nice."

Chapter Forty-One

A week later Wanda knocked on Shari's door just as the movers wheeled a stack of boxes out on their dolly. She called out the young woman's name and found her in the bedroom loading hanging clothes into a cardboard wardrobe.

"Hi, Shari. I heard you were moving to Fort Worth, so I wanted to tell you best wishes."

She stopped and smiled broadly. "That was nice of you, Mrs. Warner."

"I heard they let you out of your lease."

"God moves in His perfect timing. A couple wanted to move in this month, and they are taking over the remainder of my lease." She winked. "He has been a salad chef for fifteen years but was laid off when that chain of cafeterias went bankrupt. His whole family lives in the Metroplex so he didn't want to leave this area of Texas. The owner of one of the largest organic farms told Collin about him and he's hired him as supervisor over the fresh produce and meat sections. They plan to go totally organic."

"Good news."

Shari's smile increased. "This new guy is also going to help Sally expand her menu and create some amazing specialty salads on commission. Sally is thrilled."

"Fabulous." Wanda grinned then cast her eyes to the floor. "Listen, Shari. I'm sorry I doubted your conversion and desire to stay clean."

"Now that I know about the ups and downs you've had with your own daughter, I understand. I'd love her phone number. Maybe I can help her."

The girl's generosity jabbed Wanda in the heart. Why had she not seen this sweet side of her before? "I will, thank you." She wrote it down on the back of a receipt from Sally's Salad Bar she dug out of her wallet and handed it to her. Then Wanda took a deep breath and began the speech she'd practiced all the way over there.

"God has taught me a humbling lesson through this experience. I shouldn't have judged you, but I should have prayed for you instead. I will now as you begin your new career."

Shari's eyes glistened. She whispered a thank you.

"Here. Please accept my apology and this small gift." She gulped down a wave of emotion and handed the girl a gift bag. "I think I captured your colors. Greens, oranges, and yellows, right?"

"Uh, huh." Her eyes became round and wide as she took Wanda's present.

Wanda bit her lip as Shari dug through the tissue paper and pulled out a hand painted plaque made of crate wood with vegetables grouped in each corner. In the center was a palindrome.

Shari sniffled as she held it up. "*Live on, no evil.* It's perfect. Thank you."

They hugged then Wanda waved goodbye as she weaved through the moving crew and descended the stairs.

As she walked to her car, she noticed Todd leaning over his railing.

"You gave it to her?'

"Yeah. It was easier to paint than I thought. I've been needing a hobby."

"Other than sleuthing?"

She ignored him. "Thanks for helping me find the vegetable pattern online. Who knows, I might make some more plaques in time for the annual church festival. Think they'd sell?"

He laughed. "Of course. Everyone in town knows you have a way with words, Aunt Wanda."

Acknowledgements

Again, I feel so very blessed to have Write Integrity Press as my publisher and Marji Laine Clubine as my supporter. Thanks to Shirley Crowder who so carefully edited and put in her comments to make the story even better.

In each of my mysteries I try to place a message. This one has two. First, drugs can destroy relationships and affect many innocent people in the families of the dealers and addicts. The second is more important. No one is beyond the healing grace and mercy of Christ, our Lord.

Addiction is a fallout of the sin of Adam and Eve. It is a human condition way too many have, be it drugs, nicotine, alcohol, chocolate, carbs, sex, or video games. Some people crave being the center of attention. Others crave the adrenaline rush of drama, anxiety, and chaos. Negativity seems to be more of a pandemic than any mutant virus.

Some addictions are more socially acceptable than others, but all lead to a deterioration of the human mind, body, and soul. They draw the person into a shackled state of guilt, fear, and dependency, and away from the freedom that can result by asking for forgiveness of their sins.

We all need healing. We have all *sinned and fall short of the glory of God* (Romans 3:23 NIV). That is why we need a Savior, one who walked this earth and knows our temptations, sorrows, fears, and short comings. But more than that, He loves us and wants to heal us. And He has the power to do so.

If you suffer from any form of addiction, please seek out an understanding, faith-based counselor or an empathetic pastor.

May we all bask in the mercy we don't deserve but so desperately need.

About the Author

Julie B Cosgrove developed a passion for words at a young age. She began with word search puzzles. Then she solved the word games in the daily newspapers. She and her mother shared many fun hours playing Scrabble and Hang Man.

Then, another passion developed—whodunnits. She loved the Charlie Chan, Sherlock Holmes, and Hercule Poirot movies that played on Saturday afternoons on TV. Nancy Drew and the romantic mystery novels of the late Mary Stewart and Victoria Holt kept her eyes dancing over the pages through her school years.

Later in her adult life, her passion for Christ spurred her to write faith-based fiction and devotionals for several publications, which she has been doing since 2009. Her blog, *Where Did You Find God Today?* now has readers in over fifty countries.

But her passion remains mystery, the cozier the better. Now, she has mysteries stacked up on her watchlist on Britbox and a long list of cozies on her e-reader's to-be-read list.

She loves to write them as well.

Her first cozy, *Dumpster Dicing*, won Best Mystery by the Texas Association of Authors in 2017. She has three series published—The Bunco Biddies Mysteries, The Relatively Seeking Mysterics, and this new series, the Wordplay Mysteries.

You can find all of her fiction and nonfiction books as well as her blog's link on her website, www.juliebcosgrove.com.

Suspense & Mystery from Pursued Books

www.ingramcontent.com/pod-product-compliance
Lightning Source LLC
Chambersburg PA
CBHW070315260626
47160CB00003B/849
* 9 7 8 1 9 5 1 6 0 2 1 1 6 *